SEARCHING FOR JULIA STONE

Deborah Monk

Raven's Wing Books
Peterborough, NH

SEARCHING FOR JULIA STONE
By
Deborah Monk

© 2012, Deborah Monk. All Rights Reserved.

This is a work of fiction. Names, characters,places, and incidents are products of the author's imagination or are used fictitiously. Any resemblance to actual events, locales, or persons is entirely coincidental. No part of this book may be reproduced in any form or by any means, electronic or mechanical including photocopying, recording or by any information storage and retrieval systems, without the written permission of the copyrightowner or the publisher.

Soft cover: ISBN-13 9781618070104
Hard cover: ISBN-13 9781618070111
Kindle (mobi): ISBN-13 9781618070128
Nook (ePub: Sony Reader and Ipad): ISBN-13 13 9781618070135
Generic (PDF): ISBN-13 9781618070142

LOC Number: 2011943014

.

Cover and Interior Design:
Pamela Marin-Kingsley, Far-Angel Design

Ravens' Wing Books
an imprint of Briona Glen Publishing LLC
ATTN: Customer Service
PO Box 3285
Peterborough, NH 03458-3285
Email: customerservice@brionaglen.com
Web site: www.brionaglen.com

To my Mother,
who told me I could be anything I wanted.
And I believed her.

Acknowledgements

There are a number of people who have assisted the author along the way in making this book a reality and my thanks go out to all the people who believed in and supported me. I would also like thank the staff and consultants of Briona Glen, for working so hard to bring this book into being: Pam Marin-Kingsley, Dana Blythe, and Jason Reilly, Tammy Andrew, and Wil Birch.

Chapter One

*T*his isn't my life.

That's the first thought I've had every morning for the past I-don't-know-how-long. I squeeze my eyes shut, hoping I'll fall asleep and wake up on the right side of my life but my conscious and subconscious do battle and I lay in limbo.

Cue second thought. *I have a great life.*

Oh goody. Guilt has shown up before breakfast.

There's nothing wrong with my life. It's me. There's something wrong with me.

And that gets me to wondering... can I divorce myself? I grab the sticky pad I keep on my bedside table and start writing.

I, Julia Stone, being of unsound mind and body, want to divorce abovementioned on the grounds of irreconcilable differences.

I read it again. Simple. To the point.

But maybe a little antiseptic.

I, Julia Stone, being of unsound mind and body, want to divorce the plaintiff, aka me, because I can't stand her anymore!

Much better.

I put the sticky pad back on the table and pull the blanket over my cold shoulder.

Michael, my boyfriend of four years, wedges his back against mine. It's cozy and claustrophobic at the same time. He says I'm too dramatic.

I say I'm not dramatic enough.

I stare at the walls, making a mental note, for the umpteenth time, that the hydrangea blue walls are just a shade more purple than I wanted. Instead of making me think of spring with soft blue walls and a buttercup yellow comforter, I wake up with the urge to put Pepto Bismol in my coffee. You'd think there would be a simple light blue paint at the hardware store. There's Robin's Egg Blue, and Seafoam Blue and Bali Blue. How about giving a busy woman a break and calling a paint something like, oh-I-don't-know—Light Blue? I can't tell you what's wrong with it, but I know it's slightly off.

Katie knocks on the door and pushes it open without waiting for an answer. My tween daughter—a term I thought stood for early teenager but now know stands for Sybil-like-personality-changes-that-are-as-dangerous-as-a-great-white-shark—crouches at the foot of my bed, waiting for me to sign her note. I look at it, blame the early morning light for the fact that I can't quite read it, and pretend to look it over. I figure if it's a note telling me she's failing out of school, or that she got detention for some hormone-induced crime, Katie'll fidget. I stare at her over the paper, waiting for a guilty sign, kidding myself that I can still read her. She sighs, the quintessential sound of adolescence, and points to the line I'm supposed to sign.

Katie's a good kid... so what if I just gave her permission to skip gym? She pulls the paper out of my hand a little too quickly and starts out the door, mumbling about not forgetting to pick her up. I want to ask where and when but can't bear the thought of one more sigh clouding the room.

I look around the baseboard for the Alice in Wonderland portal that will transport me to the much more exciting and glamorous life I had every intention of growing up and into. But, no. The damn hydrangea blue wall is solid; no magic holes there.

I wiggle around, trying to get comfy. If I could just sleep for five more minutes—

Something scratches my leg. I reach down and find my very official divorce paper stuck to my ass.

I yank the paper from under the covers and throw it on the floor. All my gyrations have woken Michael. He rolls toward me and rubs my neck for two point five seconds, which is supposed to turn me on like a Mercedes, able to go from zero to sixty in under three seconds. "Hon, want a quickie before work?" he asks.

Is he serious?

Wait, maybe I've tucked passion somewhere in this coffin of a body.

Nope.

"Sorry, I don't have time," I say. Or inclination. Or desire. The only thing I want is to find the damn rabbit hole.

"C'mon. Katie's left for school. And it's been a week."

Jeesh. The electrician is coming later this morning. He could make the same argument for sex. Will I give in to him, too?

The feminist in me knows having sex when you're not in the mood is wrong, but I give in anyway. Why? Because sex will only take ten minutes and an argument would take much longer. Since I've got a civil war going on inside me, I don't have time to be side-tracked by an argument.

Michael rubs my back. I remember loving that. I remember arching into his touch, so it's easy to go through the motions, like Harrison Ford doing another Indiana Jones movie. Not an Oscar winning performance on either of our parts, but good enough returns at the box office to justify the performance.

Michael starts breathing heavier and I match his breath. Maybe if I wiggle around more I'll still have time to run out and get a cup of cinnamon coffee—who cares if it costs more than my blouse? After all, a woman's got to prioritize.

It isn't that the sex is bad. Or good. Or anything. It's like the screaming in my head has made me numb to everything else. *Find your real life*, I hear echoing in my head, like the eternal last sock lost in the dryer, going round and round with every other load of laundry, constantly looking for its lost mate. It's like *who I am* is tumbling around in the dryer of life... searching for me.

I moan, which Michael takes as encouragement to continue doing what he's doing. Although I appreciate the effort, it will take more than a little tongue action to get me going this morning.

Thirty-eight isn't old, I tell myself—a mantra that has lost its shine.

It isn't young either, a sardonic whisper caresses my skin, kissing me with its foul breath.

Shoving the insidious thoughts aside, I take a long, slow breath, yoga's promise for finding your way into the moment. Long breath in through the nose...Michael's head fits into my neck like our very own nook and cranny and I smile. My grandmother had loved the "nooks and crannies" in her English muffins and I never knew what they were. Long breath out through the mouth... Maybe I should write a sex manual. Instead of the Joy of Sex, it could be the Nooks and Crannies of Sex. Forget multiple orgasms; Chapter One would suggest bringing butter and grape jelly to bed, multitasking for today's busy woman.

He kisses my neck for a while, almost as though he knows that might be the only part of me that is paying attention to him. My libido tingles like a long forgotten limb that has fallen asleep, but I gladly squash those feelings. I have more important things to contemplate than my misplaced sex drive... like how the hell did I get here? Bored out of my cotton-picking, who-the-hell-am-I-but-please-let-me-be-anybody-but-me, mind.

Michael moves on top of me and I make the necessary adjustments, a leg here, an arm there. Holding him close, I am grateful that my body is following his lead while my mind races.

I don't like boredom. I don't like middle of the road. Growing up with an alcoholic father set me on the road to chaos. I grew up with the idea of escaping, like a puppy straining on a leash. I didn't know exactly what I was going to do with my life; I just knew it was going to be fabulous.

At eighteen, I moved to New York. Dance requires certain things that I knew a lot about.... addiction, which I got from my father; an unbelievable work ethic, which I got from my mother;

and a talent that was all my own. With those three things and my trusty old tap shoes, I spent the next decade completely and passionately devoted to my craft, my own birth into who I was meant to be. I fell in love with Richard, the only straight guy in our company (contrary to Mom's opinion, which didn't change even when we got married and had Katie). Our romance had all the elements of Cinderella that eroded into a Greek tragedy.

Incredible ups, and equally amazing downs. But I wasn't bored.

At the ripe old age of thirty, I knew it was time to retire from show dancing, divorce Richard, and put my life together. Recognizing I had a daughter and not enough money to support us, I moved home to Boston, opened a studio and worked my butt off teaching young girls to tap dance.

At thirty-five years old, I sensed a midlife storm on the horizon, so I did what any reasonable woman would do. I moved in with my boy-toy and tried to have a baby.

Bored, I was not. Miserable, moody and hormonal as hell. But not bored.

Apparently, my midlife crisis, although patient, has decided her time has come. She wants my attention and she wants it now. And I'm too tired to run anymore.

Michael is finished and I paste a smile on my face. So what if I missed foreplay and the main event? If I don't start paying attention, I'll miss the roughly three minutes of obligatory cuddling. I roll over and he puts his arm around me. I synchronize our breaths, my yogic contribution to our mating.

I have to admit, though, that if it had ever occurred to me that I was going to have a midlife crisis, I assumed that I would do that with as much gusto as I had done most things. I would quit my job, go off on a worldwide soulful journey and write a book about it, with Julia Roberts playing me in the movie.

But no. I am condemned to a midlife crisis of boredom. How mundane. How mediocre. How insulting.

Even my midlife crisis is anticlimactic.

I follow Gabriel the chiropractor into exam room three. He's the only Gabriel I've ever known. Michael and I had agreed if we had a boy, we would name him Gabriel. It's the kind of name that could be anything. Gabriel the Astronaut, Gabe the Football Player, Gabriel the Macho Pianist.

"So, you think I should take a month off?" I ask as I lie on the exam table.

"You ask me that every time you come here," he says, putting the electrodes on my shoulder that are supposed to relax the muscles. The involuntary little spasms feel like mechanical bugs are crawling under my skin. Oddly enough, I find it comforting to give up that tiny bit of control.

"I know," I murmur, resigned. Just like I asked the acupuncturist I saw, and the herbalist, and the psychic before that. None of them answered yes. Obviously, I was most disappointed in the psychic. Talk about a leading question. The others all promised their particular specialty was all that I needed to feel like myself again.

So far, no one had poked, prodded, or supplemented me back to who I wanted to be.

"Have you been doing the stretches I showed you?"

I nod enthusiastically. Of course I am... *not*. "I think I have CFS," I say, my voice muffled in the tissue covered pillow.

"Chronic Fatigue Syndrome?"

I sit up, sending my muscle stimulators flying. "You agree?"

"I'm just confirming that's what you meant," he says, replacing the little buggers that fell off.

He flips through my chart. "When you went for your physical, it says here they checked your thyroid."

"Thyroid-schmyroid. In the book I just read, it said a normal thyroid test doesn't mean everything is fine."

"You probably need a rest. A vacation. Don't you close the studio over school break?"

I sigh. "Yeah."

"A week off will be good for your shoulder."

My phone vibrates, tickling my chest. I swore I would never be one of those people who have their phone attached to their belt like a cyber umbilical cord. Instead, I tuck it in my bra. According to Oprah a few weeks ago, the fact that I can fit a gadget in my bra is a sure sign that I am wearing the wrong size. Go to a store and have a real bra fitting is on my list of things-I'll-never-get-to.

Apparently, Gabriel can feel it through my back. "You're supposed to shut that off when you come in here," he says.

"What if the President needs to reach me?"

"Answer it," he says with a sigh. "You won't relax enough for me to adjust you anyway until you check it."

I pull the phone out of my bra and read the text. "Shit! I forgot!"

"What?"

The electrodes scatter around me as I jump up. "I've got to go. My lifelong dream is being delivered in half an hour!"

It is eleven o'clock, Tuesday morning, and I have officially made it. I hand the carpenter his check and I am grateful when he leaves me alone, promising to be back first thing in the morning to begin installing the wood floor. He's already hung the spotless mirrors on the south wall. A Bose sound system, complete with four small speakers, hangs discreetly in each corner of the room. The smell of the stacks of red oak permeates the room.

A practice room.

All my life I have wanted a practice room. A place I could go first thing in the morning, still half asleep when choreography ideas spring from my sleep but never last quite long enough to get to the studio. Or at night, one last dance to put myself to sleep.

I'm not sure what to do first. Put the music on. Put my tap shoes on. Dance without either.

I have wanted this all my life.

And now I have it.

I think I'm afraid to believe it's true. I move around like a stranger in my own house. In my own studio. It's like I've never danced before. Like I haven't spent a good portion of my waking hours since I was five years old in a studio just like this.

Having imagined this moment so many times, I walk in a daze to the brand new stereo. I put in my favorite John Mayor CD—none of that typical piano tap music in my personal studio. This is my space, just for me.

I stand in the center of the room. A primal scream rises up from my untapping toes, spirals its way up my unstretched body, and bounces off the walls like a ballerina on speed.

I am crying.

And I can't stop.

Chapter Two

My therapist, Nancy, moved to Hawaii last year. When she left, she gave me her associate's business card. I was sure I wouldn't need it.

Lucky for me, my subconscious thought different and kept the card. And this morning when I couldn't stop crying, my subconscious remembered where I put it. Apparently, my subconscious could also call, book an appointment, and drive me to the medical building because now I'm sitting in her waiting room. The secretary offered me my own box of Kleenex when I checked in, but she keeps glancing at me as if she's never seen a grown woman cry. You'd think she'd be used to it.

I want to tell her the only reason I'm here—well, besides the obvious that I can't stop crying—is that my best friend Charlotte is away on vacation. I encouraged her to go to help her get over the married bum she had been seeing. Good timing for her to go away. Bad timing for me. Because without my best friend, I'm back to needing a therapist.

Nancy was a godsend. I often thought of her as my emotional mother. The time I saw her after I miscarried, she actually had me sit on her lap. Even though I weighed twenty pounds more than she did and was six inches taller, I curled up on her lap and cried like a baby.

I'm hoping Nancy's twin is on the other side of the door, her arms open, her lap waiting, and her schedule clear for the next three years.

Instead, Tinkerbell opens the door and gestures for me to come in.

I am so shocked, my tears stop for a moment.

How the hell is this tiny woman, who couldn't ride the big roller coaster on a good day, going to save me? Does my insurance know they're paying one hundred and fifty dollars to a Disney character?

"Julia?" She shook my hand. "I'm Madelyn LaPointe. Would you like to come into my office?"

Unless you've got a magic wand that I can use to cut off everyone's head, my own in particular, not on your pixie little life.

But my tears have stopped. It seems anger, the injustice of it all, is enough to piss me off just enough to make me stop crying. Her blue dress swirls around her legs, polka dots floating across the soft material like happy little bubbles. What professional woman wears polka dots? Clearly, only a therapist who hasn't had life kick the shit out of her. Well, maybe I'll just teach Little Miss Perky a thing or two. "Oh, yes. I'll come in," I say, thinking life should have forewarned her. If she wasn't going to comfort me, then I was going to find comfort in popping her proverbial bubbles.

"I'd like to take a look at your old files," she says, handing me a clipboard, "but I need you to sign this release form."

I take the form and sign it, figuring it is just a formality anyway. All the therapists in the office probably read each other's files after work, trying to find the craziest patients, the funniest, or the ones they could write papers on. That's what I'd do if I had to listen to people whine all day.

We sit in matching purple velour chairs. "May I ask you a question, Ms. LaPointe?"

"Certainly. And you can call me Madelyn."

"Okay, Madelyn. How old are you?"

"Thirty-three," she answers.

"You're thirty-three?" That took some of the wind out of my sails. She wasn't that young at all... thirty-three...only five years younger than me. Tears claw at the back of my throat.

"So you want to tell me what happened this morning?"

I sit there, not knowing where to start.

"You told my secretary that a contractor was at your house and that when he left you couldn't stop crying."

I shrug. "Well, yeah, that happened."

"Everyone knows home construction can be very frustrating."

"It wasn't home construction, really. He was dropping off the supplies to build me a dance floor. My aunt gave me an early inheritance, ten thousand dollars, and the only caveat was that I had to spend it on myself."

"Do you cry every morning?"

"Do I call you every morning?" Okay, maybe sarcasm wasn't the best path toward mental health, but really...

Madelyn sat there, apparently waiting for me to answer her question.

"No, I don't cry every morning."

"So what made you cry today?" she asks softly. "And why are you still crying?"

How can I still be crying? Shouldn't I have run out of tears sometime in the last two hours? "I don't know why I started crying. I don't know why I can't stop."

"First things first," she said. "It's okay if you cry all day. You can cry here, you can keep crying, and you can go home and still cry."

"That's your professional advice? That I just walk through my life crying?"

"I'm not advising it. I'm letting you know it's okay."

"Well, I don't think anyone else will believe it's okay. I think my boyfriend will be upset if I add tears to the lasagna. And when my daughter tries using the old excuse 'my mother cried all over my homework'—"

"Maybe worrying about everyone else is part of what got you here today. There's obviously a part of you that needs to cry right now. And you can shut it off—"

This is what I came for. The magical elixir to regaining control. "How?"

"You can try to stuff it back inside, but I'd say your tears have been stuffed inside for a long time. That's why there are so many of them."

No magic. I fall back into my chair.

She looks at the personal forms I had filled out. "So, you live with your daughter, Katie, and your boyfriend—"

"Michael. He's much younger than I am."

"Do you think I need to know that?"

"I don't know. You wanted to know his name."

"Okay, so his name is Michael and he's ... how much younger than you?"

"Nine years."

"And how old is your daughter?"

"She's fourteen."

"A teenager. That's certainly tough."

Madelyn probably thinks I'm an unfit mother for living in sin when I have a child. "We moved into Michael's house three years ago when Katie was starting middle school. The school system is much better than the town where we lived before. So there were a lot of good reasons to move in together."

"Julia, I'm not judging you."

Yeah, right. "We were going to get married last year when I was pregnant but then I miscarried and it kinda ruined the mood."

"I'm sorry," she says.

I reach for a tissue, stalked by tears. "It happens. I already dealt with this with Nancy last year."

She studies me for a minute, then looks back down at the form I filled out. "I see here you're a tap dancer."

"Yes, I teach. I have my own studio."

"So overall, Julia, how would you say your life is?"

Suddenly, I can't speak. The floodgates have opened again.

My nose is running and there aren't enough tissues in the world.

"Okay, Julia. Do you realize that while you were talking about your family, your tears were just a trickle. But when I ask you about your job, it became more like a river. And when I asked you how your life was, it was like a tidal wave of grief came into the room."

I start crying harder. "I have nothing to grieve. I have a great"—hiccup—"life."

"You agree a wave of emotion came over you, right?"

I nod.

"Grief? Anger? What would you call it?"

"Insanity. Mental breakdown. Something in me is broken, and nobody believes me."

She leans forward, not touching me, but moving a bit closer. "I believe you."

That makes me cry harder. She gives me a pillow and I clutch it to my chest. The last shred of dignity holding me together breaks and I cry for real this time, the sobbing, can't-breathe-my-heart-is-breaking crying. All the safety pins and the glue and the masking tape that I had used throughout my life to patch myself together came undone and I cried, somewhere between a minute and eternity.

When there's nothing left but some ragged, worn out breaths, Madelyn asks gently, "Julia, when was the last time you knew what you wanted?"

"I've wanted the floor forever."

"When was the last time you really wanted the floor? Not just remembered wanting it, but really wanted it?"

"I don't know. I just always thought, that's how I'll know when I've made it. Not by being in big plays, and not by having my own studio. But having my own floor, dancing just for myself; that was when I was going to know I'd made it."

"There's nothing more terrifying than 'making it.'"

"Why? I should be so happy."

"First, there's the disappointment. Usually, "making it"

doesn't quite match what we expected." She smiles gently. "And then there's the dreaded question that comes with making it... now what?"

"No one warned me there was a sequel to making it," I say.

"Okay... so last time you wanted the floor?"

"I just told you it's been a dream all my life."

"Then you must remember the last time you wanted it."

"You're not listening—"

"Was it when you booked the contractor who built the floor?"

I looked at her helplessly, honestly not knowing the answer. I miss Charlotte. She would get me a warm cup of coffee instead of barraging me with all these questions I don't want to answer.

"Okay, new question. What do you want now?"

"What do I want now?" I ask, repeating those five words like they are heresy. "I don't have time to want anything now."

"That's right. Because you are too busy doing what you think you should do."

"What's wrong with that? I love Katie. And I love Michael."

"I'm not saying you don't."

"It sure sounds like it."

"What I'm saying is that you can't really love them, you can't really know them, when you don't know, and love, yourself."

"That's the best you've got—I need to love myself more?"

"To say more would imply that you love yourself some now."

Ouch... Tinkerbell has a sting. "My self-esteem is just fine."

"I'm not talking about self-esteem. Or confidence. You obviously are quite capable, and you know it."

"I've had a great life. You know the old saying about going to the grave having used every drop of life God gave you? Well, I've done that. My eulogy is complete. If I was seventy and closer to checkout time, I'd be fine with it. I'd sit back in my rocking chair with my photo albums on the table and chocolate on my lap. But I'm sidestepping into my forties and I swear, if I have to be this frustrated for the next forty years, I'm going to kill myself."

"Have another incredible life then."

I droop further into the chair. "I'm too tired to do it again."

"Then don't think about a new life. Think of just one thing you want now."

"I don't have time to want anything now. Wanting something will be just one more thing I have to do."

"Because you're doing what you <u>thought</u> would make you happy," she said again.

"Exactly. What's wrong with that?"

"Nothing," she says softly. "If it's working."

"But that's what we're supposed to do," I cried. "Figure out what we want and then go after it."

"Yeah, but no one told you what it was going to be like when you got there. All that planning and working, where did you think it was going to get you? I'm guessing being here in my office wasn't part of your plan."

"I thought I was on the fast track to my own personal happily-ever-after, dance floor and all."

"Yes, you were. We used to teach our girls that getting married and having kids was going to make each and every woman happy. Then we smartened up and added careers, and unbelievable amounts of stress, and we now teach our girls you can have anything you want, be anything you want, it's all up to you. With that amount of choice and so little real advice or training, I think every little girl is bound to get lost."

"So now what?"

"First we have to pull you out of the game."

"What if I don't want to get out of the game?"

"Then I'll be happy to teach you."

"Teach me what?"

Madelyn has a devilish gleam in her eye. "How to become a quitter."

"You're just full of fun and games, aren't you, Tinkerbell?" I say, not meaning to say my nickname for her out loud. Or maybe I do.

"You tried the fun and games. You just spent ten thousand dollars on a dream you haven't had since you were a kid. My advice?"

"Besides quitting?"

"Get your money back and figure out today's dream."

Chapter Three

I walk through my practice room, ignoring the bundles of wood leaning up against the wall like matchstick soldiers, all standing at attention. Are they defensive or offensive soldiers? Only one thing is certain—they aren't getting laid anytime soon.

I glance in the hall mirror, glad to see that my face had lost the look of a bruised tomato. I had driven around for an hour after my appointment with Madelyn so no one would know I had been crying. During the drive her question had whispered through the car like stale cigarette smoke—what do I want now? It seemed like a simple question, but I'll admit, I was glad when I pulled into the driveway and could distract myself from the empty silence in my head.

Michael has Neil Diamond blaring on the stereo as he moves around the kitchen. He reminds me of Tom Cruise from that movie *Risky Business*, except that he has all his clothes on, which is good since Katie is upstairs, her music competing with his.

Today they seemed almost in harmony, the bass of her music shaking the walls on their very foundation and his music providing a softer melody. More often, though, they feel like two bulls inside my head trampling through the corridors of my mind like the bulls in Spain, a congested panic with nowhere to go.

Feeling like a voyeur in my own house, I watch him move around the kitchen. I love the way he moves—quick, concise, efficient. I had met him when one of the ballet teachers at my studio got married. She had brought her wedding party in to teach them all the basic Foxtrot. Her brother, Michael, was the only one without a partner and she asked me to fill in. Dancing in a man's arms was so different than tap dancing alone. Of course, I picked up the steps quicker than he did, but it was such a relief to let go, to not be responsible. I often say I fell in love with him that first night. On good days, it sounds romantic. On bad days, it sounds desperate.

"Hey, Hon," Michael says, seeing me when he turned around.

I smile. At least I try to.

He gives me a quick kiss. "I'm making your favorite."

How come he knows what my favorite is when I can't think of a single thing I want to eat? I lean over the pot. Stew. We had bought a cook book on one of our first dates and made this stew together. Hadn't I picked a new favorite in four years?

"Do we still have the book?" I ask, nonchalantly leaning against the counter. "Maybe we should pick something different."

He looks hurt. "When you called and said you were going to be late, I stopped and got the ingredients we need for stew," he says. "If we pick something new, we won't have everything we need."

Of course not. Silly me. What was I thinking? You can't just open a cook book and cook something—if I hadn't already decided I was crazy for spending half the day crying, clearly I'd be found off-my-rocker for suggesting such mutiny in the kitchen.

"We could try something new tomorrow," he adds.

"No, it's fine," I say, knowing tomorrow we'll have leftover stew.

"I'll stop and get those biscuits from the bakery that you like. They were already closed when I went by today."

Here I am complaining and he was going to drive five miles just to get the biscuits I like. Clearly I need to add ungrateful to my list of crimes.

I sit at the breakfast bar and pick up a knife and continue cutting up the tomatoes for the salad that had been started in the glass bowl.

"Katie's supposed to make the salad," he says, his tone obviously trying to tell me something, "but then the phone rang."

When I didn't pick up his hint, he couldn't help himself. "One of her friends called, she screamed something like, 'Oh My God,'" his best imitation of a California valley girl even though we live in New England, "and ran up to her room."

I take a slow breath, hoping he'd drop it.

"You really shouldn't finish it for her."

Yeah, right. Because I'd rather have Katie come downstairs either all excited, or in tears, about the latest drama in middle school. And one reminder from Michael that she left a chore undone is going to convince her that we are only here to make her miserable. Never mind we are cooking a healthy meal because we love her. No. Asking her to finish the salad is tantamount to ruining her life. Why can't Michael understand that?

"I like it when we cook together," I say, using my words to kill two birds with one stone... avoid confrontation with Katie and appease Michael all at the same time. When did I stop using my words to communicate my thoughts, my feelings, my needs? Now I seem to measure my words effectively. Effective for everyone else, that is.

"You letting her off the hook isn't right, you know," he says as he has said a million times. As an eighth grade math teacher, he thinks he has insight into kids. Half the time he's right. Probably more than half. Most times I don't care. Most times I think until you've been in the trenches with a child of your own, you don't know squat.

"I know," I say, my familiar line in the script. The words feel like rotten meat in my throat. When had I become an actor in my own life—a second rate, B-list actor, with a lousy script? Who the hell is my writer? And why can't I fire him?

I had thought that if we had a child, then he would understand that love doesn't make sense once you become a parent. That your heart and your mind will be torn apart trying to figure out the right way to parent, and they will most often disagree. Lately, I've been thinking that he wouldn't have been any different with his own child. To him, love does make sense. His heart and mind would only be more convinced that he was right.

I sigh, feeling the tears worm their way up my throat, trying to decide who I want to take on more, the self-righteous father figure or the belligerent teen.

Maybe I'll just take a shower. There's the old question: if a tree falls in a forest and no one hears it, does it make a sound? That's how I feel about crying in the shower. If no one sees you cry, it doesn't count.

I put the knife down. "I'll go see what she's doing."

As if he's recognized that by winning, he's ruined the mood, he grabs me as I walk by. "She'll be down sooner or later. How about a little dance?"

I melt into his arms. He did the foxtrot to whatever song was on and I am not going to tell him the band is clearly playing a swing beat. It feels wonderful to be moving together and quiet.

Madelyn's question weaves its way into the lyrics of the song. What do I want now? Swaying to the gentle rhythm, the question seems less threatening encased in the music.

Somewhere, echoing up from my well of tears, I hear a whisper.

Rest.

I want to rest.

The song ends suddenly and he lets me go. I stand there, lost in the middle of my own kitchen. A song shouldn't end that fast. One beat and it was over. Where was the wind-down? The afterplay? The warning? Abandoned by the music, the question and answer still taunt me.

Suddenly, I am jealous of Sleeping Beauty. I can see her lying in her glass bed, sleeping for days and months, and I want to crawl in beside her. No alarm clock, no list of things to do. Just sleep for a long, long time.

I climb the stairs and walk toward Katie's room. Who was Sleeping Beauty before she went to sleep? Was she a princess in her own right? A cobbler's daughter? An orphan? No, wait, that's Cinderella. Forget that. I already tried Cinderella on for size in my twenties. Married my Prince Charming. Somehow, we took a detour on our way to Happily Ever After and ended up in divorce court.

It seems sad the fairy tale I now most want to emulate is Sleeping Beauty. That the one thing I want more than anything in the whole world is a nap. And keep that damn Prince away from me because, I swear, I will kill anyone who tries to wake me up!

I stand outside Katie's closed door. I hear her laughing on the phone. She might as well have been on the other side of the world.

I go back downstairs and sit at the bar again, picking up the knife. "She said she'd be right down," I say. We both know I'm lying.

Michael hums as he chops the meat on the other side of the kitchen. He looks so happy. He loves living together. He's told me so. And sometimes when he talks to his friends, I hear him call me "his wife" and I can tell he is test driving the words and finding them to his liking. Sure, I can understand him wanting to get married—but to me? How is it possible that he is happy as a clam and I feel like I'm being tossed about in a tiny rowboat lost in a hurricane? With a hole in the bottom of the boat? And gray fins circling?

"I see the room's started..." Michael said.

"Yep. Bob got another project, though, so it might take a little longer." I had called the contractor after my appointment with Madelyn and asked him to postpone the floor.

Indefinitely.

Great. I'm a crazy, ungrateful liar.

Now is the time to come clean. Tell Michael that I am losing it. Tell him that although I'm sure I love him, that I remember loving him... that sometimes I don't.

That sometimes, too often lately, all I can think about is running away.

"You okay with that?" he asks, ready to jump into rescue mode. "I could call him back..."

"I'm fine," I say, cutting the carrots into tinier pieces. I scrape them off the cutting board into the pot of boiling water and watch them disappear.

Chapter Four

I walk into Madelyn's office the next day and plop down in the dark purple velvet chair. I am glad to see she is dressed more appropriately in a black turtleneck, black pencil skirt... and knee-high patent leather boots that obviously came from Street Walkers-R-Us. I decide to ignore the fact that Tinkerbell is obviously a dominatrix. "I think your idea to spend the money my aunt gave me on today's dream is dumb."

"I thought you said she wants you to spend the money on yourself?"

Why does she have to act like I am kicking the gift horse in the mouth? I am not trying to abuse it, just find a loophole. "But putting it in Katie's college fund isn't spending it. It's saving it," I explain.

"You're saving it for Katie. Isn't that just a technicality?"

I shrug. Madelyn doesn't know my aunt is like a bloodhound and I'll never get away with it.

"You know what I think?"

Here we go. Tinkerbell is sharpening her rapier wisdom.

"I think you don't have an answer. That you don't know what you want."

Should I tell her that she's made me start thinking in fairy tales and I want to be Sleeping Beauty? How can I tell her that my bones, my skin, and my blood are weary? That I want to rest more than I want to breathe?

"It's not an easy question," she says. "Next time you come—"

The look on my face stops her. "I wasn't really planning on making this a regular thing," I say.

She smiles. "That's fine. I'm here when you need me. Well, except for the end of next month. I'm going to Hawaii for a yoga retreat."

Charlotte will be home long before then.

"Anyway," she continues. "I was going to ask you to bring me a picture of yourself, of you when you remember being happy. When you remember knowing what you wanted."

"A picture of me? I'm the Mom, otherwise known as the photographer. We take pictures, we aren't *in* the pictures."

"It doesn't have to be a recent picture. It can be from anytime, when you were a kid on a swing set, when you remember being happy."

"Actually, I think I have one." I pull out my wallet and rifle through receipts for God-knows-what. "When Katie was going into first grade, she wanted to take a picture of me with her. In those days, the idea of spending a whole morning without me was tantamount to nap time without her teddy bear," I explain, finding it behind a coupon for maxipads that expired two years ago. "I had this picture of me laminated so she could take it in her lunch box. I found it hibernating under her bed with the dust bunnies." I don't tell her I kept it, hoping Katie will want it back when she goes off to college. I try to recognize the woman sitting on the white baby grand piano. I am wearing long flowy pants, a creamy white lace vest, and a smile the size of Texas.

Madelyn studies the picture. "You do look happy." She hands the picture back to me.

This person, who is me and isn't me, is grinning like she is Ariel the Little Mermaid and life is an oyster buffet. "It certainly wasn't like me to climb on furniture," I say. "I must have asked, but I don't remember asking. I don't even remember who took the picture."

"If she could talk, what would she tell you right now?"

"We don't run in the same circles," I try to joke.

"Julia..."

"I don't think she would talk to me."

"Why not?"

"Well, if I were her, and someone like me came up and said, "Hi, I'm your future," she'd just have to kill herself right then and there. And I don't think she looks suicidal, do you?"

"What would you say to her then?"

"In my ugly Mom-jeans, with my heavy face, I would hide if I saw her. I'd be too embarrassed to talk to her." I take a deep breath and glance at my watch. Plenty of time left. "You know what's depressing? Living with a happy man. And I don't just mean happy, I mean annoyingly happy. Michael walks around like everything is fine," I say, wondering if it would be inappropriate to offer to buy her new chairs for her office, more comfy chairs, since I'm thinking I'll spend my aunt's gift on therapy.

"Maybe everything is fine for him," she says, her notebook in her lap.

"And he has fun," I say, like having fun is a crime.

Madelyn pretends to look shocked.

"He works as much as I do, but he still makes time to work out. He loves it. And he loves his music. He's a DJ part-time," I explain.

"I imagine as a dancer you love music, too."

"I did. I do. I remember buying a tape or a CD and listening to it over and over again. I could listen to my favorite song in the car for an hour, the same song over and over again, and I heard something new every time."

"And now?"

"Now it seems like it's all the same stuff. I find a good CD and I listen to it once, maybe twice, and then I put it somewhere and I can't find it. And then I even forget I have it. So seeing him excited about music just irritates the hell out of me."

"I'm sure it's not easy for someone who is depressed."

I wiggle around in my chair. "I'm not depressed."

"You came to see me yesterday," she says, "because you were crying and you couldn't stop. You told me you've been searching for a diagnosis for the past two years, with naturopaths, and chiropractors, etc. I give you a diagnosis and you don't like it."

"I don't want to be depressed."

"I know you don't want to be depressed. You don't want to cry. You don't want a dance floor at your house. Seems there's a lot you *don't* want."

"Exactly."

"I imagine it's not the first time you have cried."

"Yes, it is." Remember, crying in the shower doesn't count.

"Well then, maybe repressed is a better word for you."

I toss the word around. *Repressed*. I try it on for size. "Repressed?" I say out loud like a question.

"Restrained," Madelyn explains. "Held down, kept in check."

I nod. "Repressed, like the slaves." I can live with that.

"You know who is repressing you, right?"

I can tell she's going to ruin this for me.

"You. You're the only one holding you down."

"So I'm strangling me? Got myself locked in a chokehold?"

She doesn't say anything.

"Sometimes I think I'll never find my new happiness with his old happiness around me," I say softly.

"You talk about how young he is, so how come his happiness is old?"

"Because it's my old happiness. How can I ever find my new happiness with him walking around with my old happiness stalking me, reminding me, of what I had... what I was?" I drop my head, ashamed to sound so pathetic.

Madelyn smiles. "I guess that could be annoying. But you've got to realize that he's not here just to torment you."

"Easy for you to say. I'm guessing you're not married."

She doesn't answer, but I can tell. She's not married. "I sometimes say to him that living with him is going to force me to marry an old stodger just to compensate for his immaturity."

"You know that's cruel," she says.

"Tell me about it. The old goat was never my type."

"I'm talking about you. What you said to him is cruel."

"He knows I'm joking."

She looks at me for a moment. "How can he? When you're not sure."

I lean forward. "This is what you've got to help me with. This hate. This anger. I think part of me literally hates the people I love. I know I love them. I believe I love them. I mean, I still want to love them. All I know is I don't <u>feel</u> like I love them," I confess.

"And from the sounds of it, you've having trouble faking it."

"Exactly! I don't want to be faking my life."

"How long have you been faking it?" ˙

"I don't know. That's not the important part. Fixing it, getting me back to loving them is the important part."

"Even if I could wave a magic wand and time travel you back, you'd still end up here in a few years."

"I don't want to end up back here."

She took a slow breath. "Are you trying to make Michael leave?"

"Why would I do that?"

"Do you love him?"

I start crying. "Of course I love him."

"Think this through. If he came home today, said he met someone..."

"He wouldn't."

"Okay. He is just tired of everything and he's leaving."

"I would be really surprised...."

She takes a deep breath. "Julia, just go with me. Close your eyes. He's gone. You don't even have to think about why, he's just gone."

"He died?"

"No. Because then it's not his choice and you would take on the role of poor girlfriend."

I open my eyes. "I wouldn't be the poor girlfriend. I'd be the look-how-strong-she-is-how-well-she's-handling-it girlfriend."

"Okay. What would you do? What would your life be like?"

"I'd buy a townhouse in the Newell Meadows complex. They have garages and fireplaces. And it's in the same school district for Katie."

"You know the complex?" she asks, obviously surprised.

"I've thought about it."

"You've got an escape route to your own life already planned."

"Is that bad?" I ask, leaning forward. "Or are you telling me to take it?"

"Do you want to?"

"Stop answering a question with a question."

It's her turn to lean forward. "I can promise you one thing. Your relationship isn't your biggest problem."

"It's not?"

"I'm not saying your relationship isn't in trouble. It probably is. But before we worry about that, *you're* in trouble."

"I am?"

"C'mon, Julia. You know you are."

"If we had had a baby, Michael would be the perfect dad. And then I could be the fun, crazy parent. I always said I was going to take my kid out one summer morning and teach her to eat cereal without a spoon. That's the kind of parent I planned to be. Then when Katie came along and Richard spiraled into depression, I was the only adult left and I never got the chance."

"Who says you can't be that parent now?"

"Katie's fourteen. She doesn't like anything I do. Except drive. And buy. We have a simple relationship now."

"Sounds like you picked Michael, thinking he could pick up your dropped threads. Help you put some pieces back together."

"Exactly." Maybe she does get me. "He's my second chance. I should be so grateful..." I swallow. "I mean I am so grateful..."

"It's like buying a black dress for a cocktail party, one that's more expensive than you can really afford, but you buy it for this once-in-a-lifetime party. Well, then the party gets cancelled. Do you keep the dress?"

"You want me to return my boyfriend? I know he's not very exciting..."

"You didn't get involved with Michael for excitement. You're living with him for a second chance."

Shit! When she says it, it sounds bad. I fidget in my seat.

"And worse," she says.

"There's worse?" I am horrified. There is worse than using someone you love for your own second chance?

"You think he's robbed you."

I refuse to agree with her out loud, but I don't deny it either. I do feel robbed. "It's like Michael is who I should have been with all along. Like my life got sidetracked for a decade or so, and it's finally picked up where it should be. The problem is, I kept aging during that detour and I'm not who I was. Or who I'm supposed to be."

Madelyn leans forward. "Maybe you are exactly who you are meant to be today."

I sigh and pick at the skin on my thumb. "I got my period yesterday."

"How do you feel?"

"Like I'm broken on the inside." I don't tell her that as I sat on the toilet tears joined the blood on my panties.

She is quiet, like she knows there is more.

I add in a whisper, "I also felt an undercurrent of relief."

"You mentioned that you had a miscarriage not that long ago. Maybe you're not ready to try again yet."

"I'm thirty-eight. If I don't give Michael a baby now, I'll never be able to."

"A baby isn't something you owe him."

There's no way in hell I'm going to tell her about the uglier undertow of guilt that I'm feeling. The voice in my head whispers, *Yes, you do. You do owe him.* "If that pregnancy had just been normal, I really think I could have lived my second HEA."

"HEA?" she asks.

I smile a little. "My own vernacular for Happily Ever After." My smile slips. "When you're pregnant and they tell you your hormones are off and you have to stick vaginal progesterone suppositories up there, fear invades your body. And then it's just... over."

"Maybe it won't be that way next time."

I wrap my arms tight around my body, embracing my cramps in a tight hold. "I feel loss tugging at my body, and no matter how hard I try to hold on, I'm afraid I'm losing my grip." I swallow around the lump in my throat. "It feels like the sands of time are pulling everything away from me. Like I'm being pulled out to sea and I'll be lost forever. One wrong turn and suddenly I'm rowing against the natural current of my life."

"Julia, do you want a baby? Or is it the idea of a baby that you want?"

"Yes. No. I don't know. We were using condoms, but when we moved in he just kinda stopped. And I didn't stop him. I was an only child and I never wanted that for Katie."

"This dream of another baby might be like the floor. Something you used to want. Maybe you even wanted it a lot. But I think before you do anything, you should really stop and figure out if it's what you want now."

I squeeze myself tighter, spreading cramps through my whole body. "I think it's too late."

"Too late?"

"Too late to fix everything."

Chapter Five

Therapy is for crazy people, I repeat over and over to myself as I race through the aisles of the supermarket like a squirrel in Alaska gathering nuts for an eternal winter. After therapy, otherwise known as self-inflicted torture, I cancel my evening tap classes and drive to the bookstore, buying the most exotic cookbook on the shelf. I don't need therapy. I just need to get back to the business of living. My daughter is perfectly fine, Michael makes me laugh. I have my own business. I have everything I need.

And nothing I want.

I spin around. No one is behind me in the grocery store aisle, but I swear I heard someone say, "Nothing I want" in a melodic voice. I turn back, squeezing the handle of my carriage. My purse sits in the front seat of the carriage with my laminated picture—Flat Julia—peeking out of the side pocket where I had stuffed her.

I pull her picture out—*my* picture, I correct myself. That is me, but a me from so long ago it seems a woman on the wagon trail in the eighteen hundreds would bear more resemblance to me than this smiling woman.

If you look at it from a certain angle, I decide, a somewhat annoying smile.

She certainly wasn't saying anything, this Flat Julia.

I push the picture deeper in my purse.

And I am certainly not listening.

I grab two cans of beans and go to the register, anxious to get home and make dinner for the two people I love most in the whole world.

The woman in line ahead of me has her items clearly separated on the belt… her ice cream and frozen waffles stacked neatly, then her canned goods, and last but not least, her carton of Marlboro cigarettes.

The young cashier is talking to her friend who is bagging the groceries. "My Mom's got to work on Saturday, which means I can borrow the car. Want to go to the beach?"

"I would love to have a tan for the party Saturday night," the blonde girl with the very light skin says. "You are going to Brian's, right?"

"I'll go anywhere Brian is going," the cashier says, all googley-eyed.

The girls are talking about the weekend as if it were the holy grail of possibilities…the beach, the party, the romance. Yeah, yeah. How about raking, laundry, and scrubbing toilets?

I reach for the candy rack and without looking, I grab a bag of M & M's. Not the peanut kind, the plain M & M's. The dark brown bag of candy is suddenly in front of my face, like I am a magician pulling a rabbit out of a hat. Thirty-eight and my best magic trick in life is pulling chocolate out of thin air.

Seems pathetic, and somehow necessary, all at the same time.

The girls keep talking about how much fun they are going to have. Yadda, yadda, yadda. At sixteen, these girls don't even have the slightest suspicion of what life has in store for them. It never occurs to them that they'd better expect some sour apples in the recipes of their life. They think it's going to be all peaches and cream.

Tell them the truth.

That voice again.

I zip the side pocket closed.

Why not? Tell them part of the truth.

"I never said I know the truth," I whisper in my own head since Flat Julia seems to have a direct line to my brain.

Tell that one, the cute cashier with the little piercing in her nose, that she is going to grow up and sleep on the couch most nights because she refuses to sleep beside the father of her children.

"The one that is obviously boy crazy?"

And the brunette at the next register... she's going to start drinking vodka with her cheerios just to get through the day.

"Surely someone is going to grow up happy," I say to myself with more confidence than I feel.

Sure. The blonde girl that is bagging for you? She's going to have two point five kids, a beautiful house, and one of the few really good men.

Why is it always the blonde? I joke. Flat Julia needs to lighten up.

And then her youngest child is going to get sick and die before she does.

I freeze. It's one thing to hear voices in my head, I reason. Everyone has that, right? But having a conversation with them is a whole other layer of cuckoo.

The woman in front of me drops her coupon envelope. While twenty and thirty cent coupons rain everywhere, I decide I have one more trick up my sleeve. I will abandon my shopping cart, leave Flat Julia on the candy rack between the Mars Bars and the Milky Way, and walk out of the store and disappear.

Blondie leaves her bagging station and goes to the next register. "I can help you over here," she says to me. Such a sweet girl. I want to warn her in the worst way.

Instead, I open the bag of M & M's and pour half the bag into my mouth so I can't talk. What am I going to say? Don't have the third baby—you'll be pushing your luck. It will be the beginning of the end for you. All because I am hearing a picture of myself pretending to be a fortune teller?

We move my items over to her register and I pay for them, keeping my mouth full of chocolate.

Ignorance is bliss. Remember ignorance? Flat Julia asks. *Remember bliss?*

"Ignorance may be bliss," I mutter under my breath, "but reality is hell."

The whole scene is exactly as I had pictured it. I would make dinner while Katie did her homework at the breakfast bar. She'd tell me about her day and we'd share one of those mother-daughter moments. In my vision, I'd been wearing a pretty apron, but when I get home I realize I don't have a pretty apron so I settle for tucking the kitchen towel into my pants. Needless to say, the beef hasn't sprayed a single grease drop onto the towel. My blouse, of course, is ruined.

Never mind. Katie is at the counter doing her homework. She even gives me a quick kiss on the cheek when I give her the whoopie pie I got from the bakery. I pour her a glass of cold milk. Could we get any more Hallmarky?

But the Mexican lasagna is going to take hours, and Katie is moaning about algebra, and I can't wait for her to finish and go watch television so I can pour myself a glass of wine.

Cooking is for crazy people, I realize as I cut up enough onions to burn the eyes of half of China. If Curt Schilling were pitching today, I'd be two strikes closer to crazy. Hell, therapy, cooking, and talking to a picture of myself—who am I kidding? I've already hit a home run right out of the crazy park.

Mexican lasagna had sounded like such a good idea in the bookstore. A nice combination of culture. But damn, I should have read the recipe closer before I picked it. The beef has to simmer for an hour before I can even start the damn recipe.

Katie spies the can of refried beans. "I'm not eating anything with refried beans," she says. "They're gross."

"I am going to leave them out on your half." Not true, but I've been lying to Katie about what is in her food for so long that it doesn't count. The parent bible of good health is clearly the exception to the do-not-lie rule.

Michael comes in from the garage. "What's going on here?" he jokes, coming up behind me. Like someone cooking, me cooking to be precise, is a laughing matter.

"Mom's in a bad mood," Katie says.

This from the teenage queen of bad moods? "No, I'm not."

Katie raises an eyebrow, as if that one eyebrow is the judge and jury of moods.

"Why do you say I'm in a bad mood?"

"You're acting like it."

"What am I doing?" I ask, trying to ignore my temper, which is sitting like one of the seven dwarfs on the shelf with the dinner plates, laughing at me. I turn to the other counter and start cutting up the peppers. If Katie and Michael aren't going to fit into my Hallmark moment, I'll just ignore them.

"Ah, Hon, you know peppers give me gas," Michael says.

I put down the knife. I hate them both. "At least now you'll have an excuse for stinking us out of the house," I say.

Katie reaches up to give me a high five. "Good one, Mom."

It seems the way to score a point with one of them is to cut the other one down. Nice family game.

Katie gathers up her homework. "Can I watch TV now?"

I rub my forehead and nod.

"In the middle of the afternoon?" Michael asks, like we are talking about committing some crime.

I imagine tucking a water pistol into my makeshift apron. *"Katie, you get the masks, saddle up the ponies, and we'll mosey on down to the convenience store and rob them."*

"But, Mom, my favorite soap is on."

"Now, missy, you know the rules. Robbery in the afternoon. Television at night."

"She's already done her homework," I say, hating myself for explaining. "She's got softball from five to seven, then she'll come home, have something to eat, do her reading, and it will be nine and time for bed. So a half hour of television in the afternoon isn't going to hurt her."

"How about I throw some balls and you can practice your hitting?" Michael offers.

"I'd rather watch TV," Katie says, walking off.

I start peeling an onion with a vengeance. I am the mud pit between these two as they play their tug of war game.

"I told you she's in a bad mood," Katie says over her shoulder.

"I am not!"

He shrugs, obviously agreeing with Katie.

Eggshells. All the time. Eggshells through Katie's adolescence. Eggshells with their relationship. They are right. I am in a bad mood. Walking on eggshells in your own home has a way of doing that.

The phone rings and Katie lunges for it, but Michael is faster. "Katie who?" he says into the phone, as if she doesn't live here.

"Give it to me," Katie yells.

"And you're Emily? Emily who?" he asks, as if Katie's best friend didn't call twenty times a day.

Why do they have to make something as simple as answering the phone difficult? Their voices, their games, feel like spiders walking on the inside of my veins. This little dance they do of annoying each other, sometimes I can pretend it is all a game. Other times I wonder... do they even like each other? Or do they tolerate each other because of me?

Katie wrestles the phone away from him and goes upstairs, complaining about how lame we are. Apparently, I'm lame by default.

Extra peppers. And extra beans. That's what this lasagna needs.

"Want to go rollerblading on the bike path after dinner?" Michael asks.

"Maybe," I say, which we both knew means no.

"And the Smiths invited us over to play cards."

"I've got to take Katie to softball. And pick her up."

"Do you mind if I go?"

"Of course not."

And I don't. Not really.

Okay, truth be told, I resent the hell out of it. Not the rollerblading. Or the cards. Just the fact that he still knows how to have fun, when it seems I have forgotten. You'd think once you forget something, you wouldn't miss it.

Unless you have someone reminding you every ten seconds of what it is that you are trying so hard to forget.

He gets the wine out of the cabinet. "Want a glass?"

"God, yes." I take a delicious sip of the wine, feeling it cleanse my veins.

Katie comes running downstairs. "Mom, guess what?"

Another sip. "I don't know. Emily's got a new boyfriend?" Thankfully, boyfriends at this point don't really mean anything.

Katie shakes her head. Her body is vibrating with excitement so I take a guess. "Tiffany got a haircut that is so cool you just have to go to the same salon, for the same side bangs, or you're going to die?"

Katie shakes her head again and I take another sip of wine.

"You know how Emily's family is going to Disney World over vacation?" Katie asks.

Of course they are. Probably smiling and singing songs all the way. They'd pose with Mickey Mouse and be that picture-perfect family on the postcard that no one can live up to.

"Yes, Sweetie, I know..." I say, ready to make all the excuses why we can't go this year. "Maybe next year—"

"They said I can go with them."

Sucker punch.

"All we have to pay for is airfare."

I stand there with my mouth open but nothing comes out.

Michael steps up to the plate. "Why don't you hang up and we'll talk about this."

What is there to talk about? Katie can't go to Disney World with the perfect family. She'll never want to come home. Who would blame her? Hell, if I could go with them...

"I'll call you back, Em," she says, hanging up.

Since when did she ever do anything Michael asked without arguing?

He eyes me over his wine glass. I take a deep breath. Obviously, we just need a minute to come up with the reasons she can't go.

"I've got plenty of frequent flyer miles," Michael says.

"What?" This didn't sound like a reason she can't go. "I'm sure it wouldn't be the same airline as Emily's family... and Katie's too young to fly alone."

"With the credit card miles, you can fly any airline," he says.

Since when are Katie and Michael partners?

Katie's earthquake is turning up the volume on the Richter scale. She runs over and gives Michael a hug. "Can I go, Mom? Can I?"

I can't think of a single reason to say no. I've known Emily's family for years. It will barely cost me anything. So I do what I always do. I say exactly the opposite of what I want to say. "Sure, Sweetie."

Just like with Michael, go means stay. Yes means no.

Why?

Because lying makes everyone else happy.

Katie throws her arms around me and I feel her tremors up close. I hug her tight, grateful for the contact, wondering when making everyone else happy stopped being enough to make me happy.

Chapter Six

"**D**epression is the fragmentation of the self," Madelyn says.

It's hard to concentrate on Freudian philosophy coming from a woman dressed in crocodile boots with pointy toes. Wasn't there a big crocodile in Peter Pan? I can't help but wonder—since I called her Tinkerbell out loud that one time—is the always present hint of Tinkerbell intentional? "Don't those boots hurt your feet?" I ask.

Madelyn smiles and raises a leg, admiring her boots. "I suppose if I had a job like yours where I'd be on my feet all day, then they would."

I look at her boots, with the high heels, and wonder what it would be like to sit and listen to people all day. "Did you always want to be a therapist?"

"I guess I did," she answers.

I try one of her tricks... I am quiet, hoping she'll continue.

"My mother was bipolar," she explains, "and I wanted to know more about it."

It works! "Were you able to help her?"

"She died long before I finished school."

"I'm sorry." Poor Madelyn. No mother. No husband. Well, maybe not so poor. She does have those great boots.

She crosses her legs and I can tell it's time to get to work. I pull Flat Julia out of my purse and lay her on the table, ready to admit my secret here in her bulletproof office. "I hear her voice in my head."

Madelyn leans forward like I've sprouted wings.

"Flat Julia," I admit sheepishly. "That's what I call her."

"I think it's wonderful that you're open to dialogue with your younger self."

"Why? So you can keep seeing her when my insurance runs out?"

Madelyn laughs. "I might have to enlarge the picture so she's big enough to sit in your chair."

"I don't want her around." I am lying. I am lying with canyon-deep desperation. I want Flat Julia around. Truth is, I don't want me around.

"And how do you feel about this?"

"How do I feel?" I repeat. "Isn't that Psychology 101?"

"Still seems like a good question."

"Besides the fact that I think I'm crazy?"

"Who isn't? You're crazy. I'm a cliché. So how do you feel about your younger self talking to you?"

"It's not like we're best friends or anything. Maybe I don't feel anything in particular."

"And maybe you do. Since you don't seem to know what you want, maybe you should ask her."

"I think I'm afraid to talk to her. I feel like a walking horror movie. You know, where the babysitter sees the basement door, hears the warning music, and still opens the door to the cellar where the killer is hiding?"

"Julia, most of our cellars aren't quite the dungeons of scary movies. Most don't hide monsters waiting to put our eyeballs in a candy jar. Most of our cellars have a lot of old, forgotten junk. That's why you're here. To shine a flashlight into your dark places."

I can almost feel the light sweeping back and forth across the dark recesses of my heart. For one second it threatens to shine on a dark box I've buried deep inside and I quickly point it in a different direction. "What if I already have enough voices in my head, telling me what I need to do... what I should do... what I shouldn't do, that I don't want another voice clamoring for my attention."

"When you are feeling so overwhelmed that you become frozen, maybe you should just ask the voices what they want or need. Maybe Flat Julia can help you."

"So your professional advice is to listen to Whiney, Miserable, and Helpless?"

Madelyn laughs again. "Are those some of your personal seven dwarfs?" she asks.

I nod. She's starting to get me.

"Maybe Flat Julia is your Happy."

I take a deep breath. "Fine. You want to know how I feel about her? I say I hate her, that I don't want her to be around. But the truth is, I wish I could be more like her."

"Like her how?"

"She didn't think about everything, and rethink it and rethink until she can't remember what she is even thinking about."

"So you'd like to think less?" Madelyn echoes me, urging me to continue.

"God, yes. And worry less. And be afraid less. Flat Julia thinks everything is going to work out just fine. And she's always ready to go for it."

"Can you say *I*? *I* was always ready to go for it? Because Flat Julia is you."

"*I* was always ready. *I* was willing to try anything. And *I* believed—" The tears are back, leaking out of my heart.

"What did you believe, Julia?"

"Things like 'love can conquer all'. And that love is fair." The tears are clawing their way up the back of my throat. "And that you would never, ever hurt someone you love."

"Those are nice ideals, but they aren't real, are they?"

"Why aren't they true?" My voice is cracking. "I want them to be true."

"It's the people we love that hurt us the most. The more we love them, the more they can hurt us."

My tears have wrapped themselves around a primal scream that I am constantly trying to swallow. I stand up and start pacing around her small office. "And Michael walks through life. He wants to marry me, did I tell you that?"

"Why does that make you angry?"

"Because he doesn't know. He doesn't know that life's gonna hurt, and that if we get married, I will be the one that hurts him."

"Maybe you will. Maybe you won't."

I stop pacing, my chair between us. "You just agreed it's the people we love that can hurt us the most..."

"That doesn't mean you'll automatically be the one to hurt him."

"But I will. Somehow, someday, without even wanting to be the one, I will hurt him."

"Does Katie hurt you?"

I answer automatically. "No."

She waits.

"Okay. Sometimes."

She waits some more.

"Okay, okay. A lot. But she never means it. When you get pregnant, they tell you about the baby coming out. But they don't tell you that somehow, your heart comes out, too. That it gets put out there in the world, where it's just waiting to take a beating."

"Would you give her back?"

"Of course not!" I should never have admitted this to her—she can't understand. She doesn't have kids. "Katie's the best thing that ever happened to me."

"And maybe you are the best thing for Michael. Maybe he loves you that much that he's willing to take a chance on being hurt."

He might not if he knew everything I'd done. "It's bad enough that I had to learn it," I say as I drop back into my chair. "I'm not going to perpetuate the misery and start teaching the crappy reality of life... and love."

"What does Flat Julia think of this?"

I stare at her smiling face on the table, my fingers itching to find a pencil and poke holes in her eyes. "She doesn't know these life lessons either. And I hate her. I hate her for not knowing."

"Why?"

"She saw a pot of boiling water and she jumped right in. And I got burned. Now I'm so afraid I just tiptoe around the water, sticking a toe in here, then walking around to the other side. Even if it's lukewarm, even if it's perfect, I'm afraid to jump in. I hate her for making me afraid."

"Did she know boiling water burns?"

"Of course not. It just looked like bubbles."

"So you hate your younger self for not knowing better?"

"Yes. And I hate my older self for being afraid."

"If Katie jumped into a pot of boiling water, let's say by mistake or it was an accident, would you hate her?"

"No. I'd jump in to save her."

"Who says you have to get burned to save her?"

Who says I have to get burned to save her? She is so not a parent.

"And what would you whisper to Katie on the whole ride to the hospital?"

My stomach clenches. "I love you," I whisper.

"Maybe that's all Flat Julia wants to hear," she says softly.

It sounds simple. So why do I feel so deflated that just getting up might be more than I can handle?

"We end up living trying to avoid pain," Madelyn continues. "Trying to avoid hurt. Avoid failure. So we choose to get numb."

Tink's a real downer today.

"But as an adult," she says, "you get to go forward, knowing you will get hurt. Knowing you will fail."

Getting up and leaving isn't sounding quite so hard anymore.

"The beautiful part..."

Thank God there is a beautiful part.

"...is knowing you can handle it."

"But I don't want to handle hurt. And failure."

"It's part of life."

I pick up Flat Julia and put her back in my purse. "That's why I want to be her again."

"Julia, this is what depression is. This split in yourself. You won't be happy again until you fuse all your parts back into you."

"I don't want Dingbat or Scaredy-pants back in my little gang of dwarfs. They're out."

"Then who is left?"

"Empty, Hollow, and Lonely." The bell dings, signaling my time is up.

It's Sunday afternoon and I climb the stairs from the garage to the house. Katie is over at Emily's and doesn't need to be picked up for another couple of hours. I stopped at the convenience store and grabbed some things to make a late afternoon breakfast. When we moved in together, one of the things Michael and I used to talk about was Sunday morning breakfasts. Of course, Katie's softball practices start really early on Sunday morning and although we always planned to get up and have a relaxed breakfast, (at six am... yeah, right!) we always ended up having frozen waffles, usually in the car. Today we are going to have breakfast, just the two of us. We'll make scrambled eggs and hash browns together, and we'll take the time to eat it together on the back porch with a hot cup of coffee. And we can talk about nothing. And about everything.

I push open the door into the kitchen and proceed to trip over Michael's shoes. I catch myself, but my bag falls and eggs splatter on the floor. I look at the raw scrambled eggs. "Seriously? SERIOUSLY?" I yell.

Michael comes running from the den. "What's the matter?" he asks.

Like it isn't obvious.

"Sorry about that, babe," he says, picking up one of his sneakers and the three other pairs of shoes he has strewn about the door. He throws them down the stairs into the basement.

"Great," I mumble. "Now I can trip over them again when I go out to my car."

"I'll pick them up next time I go down," he says, going into the kitchen for a towel to clean up the eggs.

I pick up the sneaker I tripped over. I try to tell myself it's just a sneaker, but it feels like a heavy symbol of everything that's wrong.

"Don't worry," he says. "We'll have pancakes instead of eggs."

"Pancakes need eggs, too," I remind him as my blood simmers in the veins behind my eyes. Its times like this I miss Katie's dad. We knew how to fight. I remember one time I threw a cake at him. A German chocolate cake, which is my favorite. One minute the cake was on the counter in front of me, and then it wasn't—it was dripping down the wall beside the front door. Richard was walking out and thought he was going to have the last word. I'm not saying throwing cakes is right, but at least there was a release. Now I feel like I'm riding a roller coaster—you know how the roller coaster climbs slowly and it builds all this tension for the drop? Well, it's like I'm going up. And up. And up. Slowly. Torturously slowly. And there's no crest. No top that I can go over and finally find out how big the drop is.

Michael picks up the gooey paper towels and carries them into the kitchen to throw them away, leaving a dripping, slimy trail of leaking eggs.

He takes one look at my face and throws his hands up. "Don't worry," he says. "I'll clean it up to your standards, Julia."

He makes it sound like my standards are impossibly high. I feel like I've compromised myself right down to the bottom of the barrel.

He wets a sponge in the sink to wipe up more of the mess. "I'll just run out and get some more eggs," he says.

As if it's that simple.

"It's not about the eggs," I say, watching him clean up. I'll be damned if I'll help clean up. "It's about the shoes." *The shoes you leave all over the place. The dirty clothes you leave everywhere. Like what I want doesn't matter.*

"I know. I'm sorry. But I'm getting better," he says with a smile I know he's hoping I'll think is cute. I'm really thinking I'd like to hit him in the face with the shoe I'm still holding. He thinks he's a happy-go-lucky guy. I think he's emotionally flatlined, and it seems the more he flatlines, the more I ride a roller coaster of up and down emotions. They say couples balance each other, and I'm starting to think it's his fault that I'm going up and down as often as I am.

"You think you're getting better at picking up your shoes?" I ask incredulously, dropping his offensive sneaker.

"When was the last time you told me?"

"Last Sunday. And the Sunday before that."

"See. Now you only have to tell me once a week."

"That's because I put them away for you Monday, Tuesday, Wednesday, Thursday, Friday and Saturday."

He looks at me. "Well, if you're putting them away, then I don't know they're bothering you."

"If they weren't bothering me, I wouldn't put them away!"

"Babe, we don't want to spend our afternoon together fighting about shoes, do we?"

He makes it sound like it's my choice. "Of course I don't. But it seems like we're going to because you leave your shoes around wherever you feel like. You live here like it's all about you.

You do things exactly how you want, and tough shit for me. So yes, I think I do want to fight about shoes."

He sits back on his heels. "How am I going to learn the shoes bother you if you do it for me?" he says, using the eighth grade teacher voice he uses to get through to hormonally insane teenagers.

"Because you love me and you should listen to me?" It seems so desperately obvious to me.

"You say a lot of things. How do I know which ones really matter to you?"

"So it's my fault you don't listen to me?"

"No. But if I can't figure out what's wrong, how can I help you?"

"I didn't ask you to help me. I asked you to listen to me. When I want your help, I'll ask for it."

"No, you won't. You'll say one thing and expect me to know you mean something entirely different."

"So you're saying if I'm clear, then you'll listen?"

"Of course."

My blood is boiling now. "Bullshit! I've been clear about the stinking shoes and there's another pair there every day."

"I didn't know it mattered to you that much."

"How can you not know? I've been telling you every week for how many years?"

I drop his shoe. "I see the shoes in the doorway and I think, 'he can't possibly love me.'"

He looks at me like I've lost my head. "You think when I take my shoes off I'm thinking I don't love you?"

"I don't think it. But I *feel* it."

"You can't feel what you know isn't true."

"Yes, I can! I can feel whatever I want." He's staying calm and I'm buckling my seat on the death-defying roller coaster again.

He picks up the sneaker I dropped. "Would it make you feel better to throw this at me?"

He thinks handing me a weapon, a weapon of his choice, and giving me permission to throw it at him is going to make me feel better?

Richard didn't hand me the cake...

Then again, our fights were one of the main reasons we got divorced, but at least he rode the roller coaster with me.

I take the sneaker from him and walk over to the window and push the screen up. I drop Michael's shoe out the window and see it lying alone in the driveway. Maybe I'll throw his other shoe away so next spring, when he finally goes looking for it, he won't be able to find its mate.

"Feel better?" he asks.

No, I don't feel better. "I don't understand why my asking you isn't enough."

"I swear I won't do it again," he says,

"You say that all the time. You will... and it's not about the shoes anyway."

"What the hell is it about then?"

"I want you to listen to me. I want you to feel something. You say you love me, but you don't even care enough about me to put your goddamn shoes away! You say you wanted a baby, but you had a friend over the night we miscarried!"

"Holy shit, Julia. Do we have to go back to that again?"

He's raised his voice, just a notch, but I feel a petty satisfaction. "Well, you did."

"I asked," he explains for the umpteenth time, like maybe it will make sense to me this time. "I asked you if you wanted to do anything. I asked you if you wanted me to cancel plans I had with Chris."

"You shouldn't have asked!"

"I'm sorry I asked. And I'm sorry I listened to what you said."

"You didn't listen!" I shout.

"You said he could—"

"I wanted you to really listen to me."

"I did."

"No you didn't! I had a miscarraige. I lost our baby! I wanted to cry. I wanted you to cry."

"How would my crying have helped you?"

"Because I would have known it hurt you. I would know you feel something."

He reaches for me, and I know I've lost him. He's back to being calm. And rational. On the surface it looks like he'd do anything for me. So why can't I get him to really hear me?

"I'm sorry," he says, getting up.

How do you fight with an apology? Even if it is for the wrong thing?

"I'll never leave shoes in the door again." He hugs me and I let him, all the fight drained out of me. We keep coming back to shoes, and that's not the issue. But if he won't listen to me about the shoes, why would I trust him to listen to anything that really matters?

Chapter Seven

There are two pleasures left in life that are all mine...

Coffee—

and Charlotte.

Today, I need both.

During a woman's life, different relationships are the main focus. First it's your parents. Then teachers. Then friends. Then boys. Then your own little family. And of course all those relationships are still an integral part of my life. But the place I feel most understood, the place I find the most comfort, the place I can really be me, is with my best friend Charlotte. I honestly don't think I could manage this muddy stage of life without her.

And she's been on vacation.

Clearly, the crying, the therapy, has all been because I've missed Charlotte. If she has to go on vacation again, I decide, I will just go with her. The money I'll save on therapy and tissues will pay for a safari.

I balance our hot coffees in my hand, a caramel machiatto for me and a soy latte with two pumps of chocolate and extra whipped cream for her, as I open the door to the Curves Gym for Women that she owns. Music pounds with a heavy beat designed to jump start the most dormant of hearts.

Charlotte is sitting at her desk, concentrating on paperwork, her wayward hair in its normal explosion around her head. She looks tanned and relaxed. The best she has looked in a year.

When I first moved back to New England ten years ago, I received a free trial to Curves in the mail and had the crazy thought that I should exercise. I've come back a couple times a week faithfully since, but never to work out. She says it was a mass mailing, but I know God made mine a special delivery and it would be greedy of me to garner a best friend and an exercise regime all out of one mailing.

Stairmaster or best friend?

Easy choice.

We chat about anything and everything. A little bell in the background of the music tells the clients when it is time to switch machines and it seems we often switch subjects just as quickly. It is a great system so we never belabor anything for too long—but it also means we can talk about the same things for years.

"Julia!" Charlotte jumps up and hugs me. I struggle to put the hot coffee on her desk, hug her, and be hugged, all at the same time. Thank God we women can multitask. "I've missed you so much!" we say, a chorus of feminine longing.

"So how was it?" I ask, sitting down and opening my coffee. "Was it everything you hoped for?"

Charlotte laughs, taking her seat and facing me. "It was great," she says. We take a sip and are quiet for ten seconds, respecting the first sip rule. Everyone knows it's the best sip of the day. Then there is no stopping us. "It was just what I needed," she says. "Out in nature for hours at a time. No phones. No television. No talking. I really got a chance to shut off. I feel rebooted."

"You look absolutely wonderful. It doesn't look like you went and spent ten days with smelly horses, working your ass off." I eye her suspiciously, picking up one of her golden curls. "More like you went to a spa and sat out by a pool. And got highlights!"

"Just from the sun, I promise."

"I want your hair," I say. "No, wait. I want to be your hair." It's true. Charlotte's hair is wild and curly, with strands going off in all directions. Mine, on the other hand ...

"You've got nice hair, too," she says, clearly reading from the best friend's script.

"I'm thirty-eight years old and I'm wearing a ponytail. Talk about lame." Straight and narrow hair, that's what I've got. "I should hang myself with this ponytail. When I was in my twenties I had really short hair. It was easier for all the wigs I had to wear in different shows. It took me two seconds to dry it, and I didn't even need a brush. Just a dryer and my fingers and twenty-five seconds.

"So cut it again."

"It took me so long to grow out," I whine. That is part of my problem in life, too. When I work hard to make something happen, it seems wrong to undo it. More wrong than living with something I don't particularly like.

"I think you'd look great with a mohawk," she says, studying me while she licks whipped cream off her lips. She makes even her coffee a dessert.

"A mohawk?" I say, pretending to consider it. Our conversations vacillate between silly and profound and back again, so many times that half the time I don't know what we are really talking about. Hair? Life? Both? I pull a paper bag from my oversized purse. "Pumpkin muffins, stuffed with cream cheese filling," I say, teasing the treats out of the bag.

"Today isn't Friday," Charlotte says, grabbing one of the muffins anyway.

"Your coming home is enough reason to celebrate. Plus, you've been exercising for ten days, literally working your ass off from the looks of it, and I've been burning stress calories. I'm afraid we're both going to melt away to nothing." Of course, she licks some of the cream filling out first. Then she'll attack the top of the muffin, and probably not eat the rest.

Me? I take a bite from the side... a little top, a little bottom, and barely any filling. "So... did you meet any dudes at your dude ranch?"

She shakes her head. "You know I didn't go looking for guys."

"You don't have to go looking for them. They seem to find you. C'mon... a mad fling with a cowboy? If you didn't have one, can you make one up?"

"Well, one night our group did go to town for country dancing. I guess you could say I met a real life cowboy."

"Seriously?" I ask, suddenly forgetting all about my muffin.

Charlotte nods. "He danced like a dream. You know I don't know how to waltz, but in his arms I became a ballerina floating across the floor. He only came up to here though," Charlotte says, pointing to her sternum.

"So, he's a bit shorter than you," I say, hungry for more details.

"And older. A lot older."

What's a few years? You never went for younger men anyway."

"And he's married. His wife had had hip surgery and wasn't able to dance. She was there though, cheering us on."

I pick up my muffin again. "Short, older, maybe, but married—"

Charlotte smiled. "I know. Been there, done that. Did I mention he's bow legged, too? Apparently that's a work hazard for a cowboy."

"Shit! One more fantasy bites the dust. Next you're going to tell me spies like James Bond—the Sean Connery type, not so much the Roger what's-his-name type—don't exist. I've only got one more fantasy for you to go out and squash like a bug until I'm fantasy free."

"The parachuting instructor one you're going to have to investigate by yourself."

I sigh. "There's something about being tied in a harness with a man, up ten thousand feet in the air, with nothing between you and the hard ground. With the wind whipping around you in a tin can of an airplane, no one could blame you for having one last roll in the proverbial hay before you jump."

Charlotte pulls off the top of her muffin, savoring the best part. "Remind me to show you the little hat I bought. I thought maybe we could make a cowgirl doll."

I smile, thinking of the doll business we've talked about starting forever. "You think we should dress the dolls we haven't even put together yet?"

Charlotte laughs. "No pressure. I think our doll business is really just a good excuse to go to flea markets." She takes another sip of coffee. "Your turn. Whad'cha do while I was gone? And how're Katie and Michael?"

"Let's see. I'll start with the obvious. Michael and I had a fight about his shoes again yesterday. I can't believe—"

"Julia, do the shoes really bother you that much?"

"Not exactly, but—"

"Then stop dancing around the shoes and talk to him." She gives me a look. That's the problem with best friends—they know everything about you. Even the things you wish they didn't.

"If I can't get him to listen about shoes..."

"Maybe he's not listening because that's not really what you want to talk about."

I hate it when she insists on skating on thin ice. "I never said I wanted to talk about anything else."

Charlotte leans forward and covers my hand. "I think secrets boil us on the inside."

"What do you know about secrets?" I ask, pulling my hand away and pretending to eat my muffin. "You're the most open person I know."

"You'd be surprised," she says, winking with mystery. "I'm just saying Michael's one of the good guys."

"If he's such a saint..."

"I'm not saying he's a saint. I am just saying that even though he's a great guy, he's clueless."

"So I've got a clueless saint?"

Charlotte laughs. "He's young, naïve, and in love. Just because he loves you doesn't mean he understands you." She takes a long sip of her coffee. "He wants to be your knight in shining armor."

"But where's the rust?"

"The rust?' she asks.

"Yeah. The rust on his suit. He never loses it. Never gets mad. And that makes me mad."

"So you want him to get angry?"

"Yeah. I want him to get mad, and storm off. And then come back and apologize. How can I believe we can get over anything, if we don't practice?" I shake my head. "But never mind our weekly argument," I say, taking another sip of coffee. "You can never go away again, at least not without me. While you were gone, I had a mini-meltdown. I was having the floor delivered for my dance room and I just started crying. And crying. So I went to see someone in my old therapist's office. I've seen ET a couple of times now."

"ET?"

"Evil Tinkerbell. That's what I call her. In my mind anyway. She seems all nice, but then she's got this sting with words. But that's last week's news," I say, gearing up. "Katie is going to Disney World over school vacation with Emily."

"Perfect-family Emily?"

"That's the one. And I'm having a really hard time with it. I reminded Katie that I always told her I was going to take her. And you know what she said?"

Charlotte shakes her head.

"She simply said, 'But you didn't'. And she wasn't even saying it fresh. Then she said we could go again. Another time. But no other time is as special as your first, when you're little, and you still believe Mickey Mouse is your friend."

"I think you missed that boat already. Katie's fourteen."

"That's not the point."

"I didn't think you wanted to go to Disney World. Didn't you say you danced there a bunch of times in high school?"

"Exactly. A terrible, dark part of me is relieved I don't have to go. Wait in those godawful lines. And she'll be so excited. It would kill me to pretend to be excited to go on "It's A Small World" one more time." I drop my head in my hands, whispering, "I'm relieved someone else is taking her. I'm a terrible mother."

"You don't have to take your daughter to Disney World to be a good mother. My mother didn't take me."

"Exactly. And I don't see any Mother of the Year awards on any of her dust free mantels."

"It certainly isn't because we never went to Disney." Charlotte shrugs. "So what you're really worried about is Katie going off without you. Having adventures without needing you, even though inside you're doing cartwheels that you're off the hook."

"Story of my life, this internal civil war. I feel like a ghost in my own life. I can see myself loading the dishwasher. Driving. Half the time when I'm driving I don't even remember where I'm going. It's a wonder I ever get anywhere." I pick up my coffee. I should have ordered a grande supersized shot of caffeine. "And I don't understand why no one has noticed I'm missing. If I had gone hiking and didn't come home, Michael would have the National Guard out looking for me. And, if I was lucky, those SEAL guys from the Navy." I try to joke, knowing I am not kidding. "Why aren't they searching for me?"

Charlotte leans forward. "Why aren't you?"

"Everyone knows the lost one isn't supposed to find herself."

Charlotte picks up the phone.

"What are you doing?"

"I'm calling the police."

"Why?"

"You want someone to make the call, to notice you're missing."

"What are they going to think when they find me in your gym?"

Charlotte hangs up the phone. "Julia, you've got to search for your own missing pieces."

"Whichever way I turn, my compass points to lost. I don't know what I'm doing, or what I'm supposed to be doing..." I sigh. "And I'm tired all the time. I've got this frantic vortex of energy swirling around in my body. Hurry up and do something. But I don't know what. It feels like the urge to do something is making me too damn tired to do anything. Carrying around a tornado is a lot of work." Again with jokes that aren't funny. "Can I wear the cool fatigue pants that I got Katie for her birthday? The ones that are way too young for me, but I bought in my size anyway, and hid in the back of the closet?"

"Of course you can. Go home, put on your cammies, and listen to a little voice inside your body."

I can feel Flat Julia stirring, but I put her back to sleep. I don't need her—I've got Charlotte.

The UPS guy comes in, dressed in his brown uniform, with his strong arms tanned from the sun, carrying a package. I whisper to Charlotte before he gets too close. "How come you get the UPS guy from the calendar?"

"I order them," Charlotte jokes, as she signs for the package and casually opens it. Her tan bleeds off her face.

"What is it?" I ask.

She drops back in her chair, her curls stirring up a pot of doom. "It's from Ken. It's a copy of his divorce papers."

Ken, the married man Charlotte had been seeing? Ken, the married man Charlotte had finally broken up with six months ago? Ken, who she was just getting over?

Charlotte just sits there, the ripped open UPS envelope flat on her lap, staring at the papers.

"They're signed three months ago," she says softly.

"What the hell?" I ask again, so many questions tossing in my mind that only one buoys to the surface... *What the hell?* "We don't care he's getting divorced. We don't care... do we?" I grab her hand and the envelope falls off her lap and lands with a thud. Apparently there is more. She continues to sit there, staring at the papers in shock, so I lean forward out of my seat, resting on one knee as I pick up the envelope and reach inside. I pull out a jeweler's black velvet box. We thought the papers were shocking. A part of me watches this whole thing play out in slow motion. My hand stretches toward her, the box resting on my palm, feeling like I have inadvertently gotten the wrong part in the play.

"What is that?" she asks, although we both know exactly what it is. I do the only thing I can think of. I flip the box open and read aloud... "Will you marry me?"

Chapter Eight

I climb the stairs in the old mill building and stop at the door to catch my breath. Ten years ago I used to race up the steps, telling my student the steep flight of stairs was a great warm up. Now I'd pay twice the rent for an elevator.

I pull the keys to my studio out of my pocketbook, which looks more like a carry on, one that technically is small enough to fit into the overhead compartment but is stuffed so full of meaningless junk that it would spill out under the seat in front of me. I'd have to get down on my hands and knees and search the whole plane for the lip plumper I bought three years ago. The balm got tired of waiting to turn my lips into Angelina Jolie's, so it blew up my purse instead.

Before I unlock the front door to my studio, I lean my forehead on the cool glass. "I am a capable, confident woman," I mumble to myself. I glance down and see a new penny, its copper face smiling stiffly up at me. See a penny pick it up, all day long have good luck. I pick it up, hoping there's some truth to that children's rhyme. The studio. My body. My face. It's all lost its bright and shiny. I drop the penny into my purse, wondering if the next time I see it, it too will have lost some of its shine.

All my life I've been striving for "I've made it." As a modern woman, I was going to have it all. And I did. I do.

And I've also got nerves that are about to snap like a rubber band from trying to hold it all together.

I walk through the reception area and look around. Maybe while Katie is in Florida I'll actually paint the studio. Every year I plan to, and every year I just end up freshening the pale peach colors it's been forever. It seems easier to coverup than to start all over.

"You're just tired," I hear Flat Julia say softly in my mind as I go through the waiting room to my office. I sit at my desk and drop my bag on the floor. "Success is its own little trap," I say as I clear my desk. "If the business was failing, I could close it. I would have to find something else to do. There is more freedom in failure. But closing the studio is like asking me which leg to cut off? Right or left? It isn't a choice I can make."

"Just admit it's a choice," Flat Julia says from the floor.

"No, it's not."

"Yes, it is," she says, obviously in an argumentative mood.

I shove my purse under the desk, hoping I won't be able to hear her anymore.

"I am a capable, confident woman," I repeat over and over as I push piles to the side of my desk and pull out a single sheet of paper. I write across the top in capital letters. TO DO LIST.

I look at it. Nah. I'm already tired. A to do list is tedious.

I crumple it up and throw it into the basket and get a fresh piece of paper. GOALS. Much better. I write on the first line. Paint the studio.

Fine. I can do that. I add a footnote... No peach!

Next.

Get estimate for updating bathroom plumbing.

Then contact landlord and negotiate having bathroom fixed. Or it's deducted from rent.

Speaking of rent, I need to call the woman who's renting my condo. When we moved in with Michael, renting my condo seemed like the perfect savings plan for Katie's college. And it would be if she paid. I add it to the list.

Fine. Next...

Catch up on student accounting.

I bite on the end of the pencil. How far behind am I? With the recital and everything, I can't really remember the last time I made a deposit.

Good point. I write quickly on the list. Balance checkbook.

If I haven't made a deposit... and the payroll is up to date or I would have seven women outside my office... so money has been going out... but maybe not in...

I get up and go to the filing cabinet and grab a chart to see how far behind I am. Three months. Three months... Three months! For all I know, none of the students have paid their tuition for the last three months. Now I am hyperventilating. I run over to my desk and open the little lock box I call my safe. Checks. Lots of checks, Thank God. I limp back to my desk, pick up my pencil... Deposit checks. Today!

If I had computerized everything last summer as I had planned...

I drop my head on my desk.

"Who's that?" Flat Julia asks from inside my purse, under my desk. Apparently she can see through furniture. Hey, if a picture can talk, why can't she have X-ray vision? "Who's who?" I say. I'd rather talk to her than deal with my suffocating goals anyway.

"The little cutie in the corner."

I look over in the corner. No one is there. I take a deep breath. *Okay, I am not here to lose it. I am here to fix it.*

"Not alone you can't," Flat Julia says, hearing my thoughts.

I laugh. "You're going to help me?"

"I will if you tell me who that little cutie is."

I figure I have two choices. I can sit here and choke myself with my goals or I can humor Flat Julia. I get up and go to the corner with the filing cabinet. The drawers are barely able to close and on top are three piles of paper that look like they played musical chairs with no clear winner.

"Behind the piles."

Of course. I shift the piles forward. Way in the back, stuck between some trophies that some little girls had forgotten to claim, is a picture of a little girl. As it happens, me. I am that little girl.

Eva had given it to me at my Grand Opening. She had obviously taken one of my childhood recital pictures to a photo shop where they somehow mounted it onto a plastic stand, and then cut out around the picture to make a standing piece, queen of the dance chessboard. "I haven't seen this since probably two weeks after we opened," I say softly, bringing the picture back to my desk and putting her on top of my goals.

"So that's you? Me? That's where we started?"

"Yup." I can't help but notice she has the same smile Flat Julia has, all bright and shiny. "She was going to grow up and become this great dancer," I say.

"You've got to admit," Flat Julia says. "You did have a pretty good run as a professional dancer."

Flat Julia—my champion? "I sure did."

"Very few people get to dance on Broadway."

"I know," I say, moving my plastic dancer around a bit on the desk the same way I did when I was five years old playing with Barbie.

"And think how few people can make a living at an art."

"I started out as a dancer. That's all I ever wanted to be. And now I dance two percent of my time, and I take care of business the rest of the time."

"Sounds like you did most of what you planned."

"I did. But now what?" Even my own little Barbie never lived in the real world. She thought you could just dance your life away. She never thought about having a baby. Having a family. Having a business. Paying bills.

"From the looks of the stacks of checks you got there, you don't have to worry about that either."

"But I'm not a dancer anymore. I'm split into so many roles in the studio that I'm coming up short in every area.

Dance director. Receptionist. Office Manager. I'm a machine. A miserable, exhausted, broken machine."

"Do what Madelyn said. Have a whole-self meeting."

I take a deep breath. "Okay. Right now I am a capable, confident woman and I am calling a meeting of my staff." I imagine my staff—i.e. all those roles that I've been trying to play—come in my door and sit on the other side of my desk. Office manager. Dance director. Receptionist.

I swallow, briefly wondering if I should get up and make sure the front door is locked. No one is due to come in this early—

"Stop procrastinating," Flat Julia says from under my desk.

"Okay." One more deep breath. "First I want to thank you all. I am grateful to each and every one of you that have been an intrinsic part of building this business. I couldn't have done it without you, and I will be forever grateful. But you were meant to be temporary. I never meant to wear all these hats for so long. And I think because so many of these parts stayed, they kicked out parts of me that I vaguely remember but certainly can't find anymore. My creativity. My solitude. My voice. Even my dancing."

Did they move on and find new homes in other people who would appreciate them? Or maybe, just maybe, if I made space for them, would they come back?

Just my luck. I call a whole-self meeting—and no one shows up.

"I think you need some props," Flat Julia says.

Why not? What's the worst that can happen: I get institutionalized for talking to imaginary parts of me?

I pull the black feather boa off the coat rack. I wrap it around my neck, pretending to be my Dance Director. "I'll go first. You need to decide if I'm a teacher. *Or* the Director. I can't be teaching twenty-five hours a week. And constantly coming up with new choreography for the advanced girls. And running the teachers' meetings where I'm supposed to inspire and improve each teacher." I wave my finger in front of my face like a true diva. "And I haven't even mentioned coordinating the summer dance camp." I sit back and cross one leg over the other with a flourish. "So I'd like a job description as one or the other. And a raise befitting my new position."

She wants less work and more money? I have to be honest. If it really was someone else in that position, I'd have to say everything she asked for is completely fair and reasonable.

This is fun.

I drop the boa and pull a tissue off the shelf behind me. I drop my new hat on my head and become my own receptionist. "You know, not giving me anything to do for three months, and then dumping three months of payments on me is too much. Each check means I have to look up that person's chart, record the payment, and make sure they're current. If they're not, an invoice needs to be printed and mailed. Then the check needs to be recorded in our books. I just need to spend an hour or two a day to stay on top of it. Of course, if you had computerized the whole system like I asked you to—"

I take the tissue off my head and tuck it into the front of my blouse, assuming the role of Office Manager. "I've been talking about that for the past five years. The problem is two-fold. Our financial manager is, pardon my expression, a bit of a wuss. And our receptionist, as she just said, doesn't like big projects."

Tissue back on top of my head. "I never said I didn't like big projects—"

Back in blouse. "You just complained about three months of payments."

The tissue flutters to the floor in the heat of the debate between these two. "Only because it's unnecessary and irresponsible. Maybe the Finance person wouldn't be such a wuss if we deposited the checks in a timely manner."

Flat Julia interrupts the argument I've gotten myself into. "Which part of this business do you like?" she asks.

"I like my coffee when I first get here in the morning." I pause, trying to think of something dance related. "And I like my five-year-olds. When a little girl puts tap shoes on, she's so excited that her shoes make noise. And they have no idea what they're doing, but the best part is, it doesn't occur to them that they're doing it wrong. And because I haven't shown them the right way yet, they think what they're doing is perfect. And they are."

"So you like the coffee in the morning. And you like the five-year-olds."

"Yup. That's about five hours of my endless week." I spend most of my time doing things I don't want to do, and then wonder why I feel so poor.

"Why can't more of your week be about the things you do like?"

"Yeah. And what if I just had sex with the Dallas Cowboys? And the Boston Red Sox, all at once."

"You think spending a lot of your time doing things you want to be doing is comparable to an orgy?"

"It's about as likely."

"You're in more trouble than I thought," Flat Julia said. "So sell the studio and ask the new owner if you can teach the five-year-olds."

"Let me go on e-Bay right now. I bet there will be a bidding war for people looking to buy a tap dance studio. And without Julia Stone, The Julia Stone Tap School isn't worth much, now is it?"

"Then get a partner."

"That's all I need. Another dancer. Talk about adding drama to the pot."

"Not a dancer. Although you obviously need to hire another advanced teacher.

A business partner."

Why does it seem no matter who I talk to, albeit all parts of me, that I argue?

"So what can we do?" Flat Julia says.

Funny, just hearing *we* makes me feel not so alone.

"We are capable, confident women—"

I jump up in my seat. "You're right!"

"I am?" a surprised Flat Julia asks.

"We need another capable, confident woman." I run over to the other desk and turn on the computer, barely able to wait for it to light up. "I am going to hire someone for the summer. I'll use half of Eva's money if I have to. Let someone else paint. Let someone else enter all the data so that our records are computerized." The computer is ready and I start typing. "Jack or Jill of all business trades needed to work over the summer, able to update a small business, from stem to stern. Responsibilities will include computerizing simple records, and hiring and overseeing contractors to paint walls and refinish wood floors."

I call the local newspaper, give them my credit card, and place my ad in the employment section. The notice will come out this Thursday and run for two weeks, with the option to renew. I just had to e-mail her the ad.

I hit send. While I am on the computer feeling brave, I send the same advertisement to Craig's List.

I hear and feel a standing ovation from all parts of me. "Thanks, Flat Julia," I whisper. This is exactly what I need. Time to rest and get back on my feet. By the fall, I'll be raring to go again.

Feeling more confident than I have in a long time, I enlarge the font, find a fancy piece of thick stationery, and print out a copy of the ad. I grab a tack and run into the waiting area. I can't help but notice as I jam the notice into the bulletin board that it looks like a ray of hope, all bright and shiny.

Chapter Nine

I climb up onto the bleachers at the school ball park just in time to see Katie swing at the ball and miss. Her long blonde hair shimmers in the sun like a waterfall cascading from beneath her helmet. Waiting for the next pitch, she sways from foot to foot. I am mesmerized by the gentle curve of her hips. It seems every time I look at her, there's more proof that my little girl is growing up.

"That's okay, Katie. Keep your eye on the ball," I yell.

She glances over her shoulder at me in the stands. I can tell by her smile that she is glad to see me. And that she wishes I would be quiet.

When she was pitching, I used to say, "No batta, no batta," but Michael reminded me that it's unsportsmanlike to put down the other team, to which I replied hogwash. In the game of life, I'm her mother and if it takes squashing another kid's ego to keep my kid afloat, then that's what I gotta do.

I finally relented when he reminded me that as the coach, he had the right to remove me from the field.

Michael is sitting in the dugout. He blows me a kiss. I know it's absolutely corny. And I love it. Mostly, I secretly love that the other mothers on the bench see it, and I know they're jealous. How could they not be? While their husbands are at work, rarely making a game, my guy is the coach. On the rare occasion that the wives are able to drag their husbands to a game, they've got their cells and their Blackberries buzzing like sand flies. One guy even brought his laptop and used a voice recording to send e-mails.

Michael asked him to put it away and stop bothering the other parents.

By making Katie and the girls the priority, even if it is only a softball game, it felt like he was our knight, able to slay all the dragons.

I watch him coach, encouraging the girls without pressure. He is tall and slender, attractive in a very natural way, but that's not what draws me to him. It's his stillness, even when he's moving, that captivates me. The irony is the very thing that makes his so frustrating to fight with is also his most attractive feature. My body relaxes when I'm near him, even when he's annoying the hell out of me. Like the other night when I made lasagna, I went to bed squeezed right to the edge of my side. An hour later, though, I woke up snuggled into him. It's like my body loves him even when my mind tells me not to.

At the end of the first inning, while our girls are heading out to the field, I go over to talk to Michael through the chain link fence. He gives me a quick kiss through the wire, and I feel like I'm in high school again, going out with the captain of the baseball team. Of course in high school, I wouldn't have been caught dead dating the captain of anything, but now I can see how it would be appealing.

"Guess what happened today," I say, not waiting for his response. "Ken sent Charlotte an engagement ring... in the mail!"

"I thought she broke it off with him."

"She did. She's so over him." I say with a little more confidence than I really feel. "She's one of the most confident women I've ever known in almost every area of life. But when it comes to love, it's almost like she doesn't think she deserves that much."

"Well, if she's going to marry him, maybe we should give him the benefit of the doubt."

"She's not going to marry him."

"Fine. Maybe I was just hoping she'd get married and get out of my way. I think if she wasn't around, maybe you would need me a bit more," he teases.

At least I think he's teasing. "You're not seriously jealous of Charlotte?"

"Of course not," he says with a smile. "Even though she does have a weekly date with you."

"Monday morning coffee is not an official date."

"Ha. You wouldn't miss it for the world."

"Okay, fine. She and I have a date." A memory of one Monday afternoon with Charlotte swarms around my heart like a killer bee, but I stamp on it quick and hard.

Katie comes over, standing a foot away from the fence in case I get the crazy idea to touch her in public. Of course I know better, but I love that she couldn't resist coming over. "Mom, stop flirting with my coach. You're like the fifth mom to think of some reason to come over here and talk to him."

"Oh, really?" I ask, pretending to be jealous.

Michael tosses her the ball. "Thanks, kiddo. I thought we agreed your mom didn't need to know about all the other women."

"Sometimes it takes other bitches coming around—"

"Don't say bitches," I say automatically. "And what do you want me to do... pee on him?"

She shivers. "Mom, you're gross," she says over her shoulder, running onto the field.

Michael shakes his head at us and starts filling in his batting order. I take a deep breath as I wander back to the bleachers. It's moments like these that I am most grateful for. Moments that seem so normal it's hard to believe anything bad could ever happen.

I text Michael. Sometimes we have our longest conversations via text at the games. "Don't you think as the Team Mom, Mrs. Smith should wear something a little less revealing?"

He texts back. "I don't think there's anything wrong with what she's wearing."

"Neither do the male seagulls that are flying into each other overhead trying to look down her blouse."

My fingers fly over my phone as I text back. "You better be careful. Someone should check the weight-bearing load on that pushup bra. If one of those underwires springs free, someone could lose an eye."

Just then, always when I least expect it, life throws me a curve ball.

A woman is slowly climbing the small bleachers, two feet away from me. Her hand is resting on her swollen belly in the way that all pregnant women have. Protective, loving, as natural as breathing.

I am frozen, but inside I am shaking. I can't stay here but there's no way out except going past her. And I can't go anywhere near her.

Michael is standing on the ground at the end of the bleachers. He never leaves the field during a game. He must have seen the pregnant woman, too.

"Hon," he says cheerfully, "do you think you could go get me a coffee? I'm falling asleep over here."

I hear his voice and move toward him. I don't care that I can't get down from this end. It is away from her.

He reaches up and I climb over the railing of the bleachers. I put my hands on his shoulders and he catches my waist as I jump down. It's only a few feet, but I think I would have jumped no matter how high it was.

He hands me some money. That's when I realize my purse is still on the bleachers. "I need my keys."

"Just take my car," he says, his arm over my shoulder.

"I can't run every time I see a pregnant woman," I say into his shoulder. Tucked into Michael's embrace, it's as if my body is home, and for just a moment, I am able to shut the door on my mind, leaving it outside where I can't hear it. While my head is tucked into the crook of his shoulder, I feel safe.

"You're not the type to run away from things," he says, always seeing a best in me that I'm not sure even exists.

"So why should I now?"

"Because it hurts you."

I can't help the tears that are filling my eyes. "That's not a good reason."

"Then do it for me."

"She's drinking coffee," I whisper. I never drank coffee when I was pregnant. Guilt bludgeons me from the inside. Obviously I had done something wrong.

"Julia, do it for me," Michael says softly.

"Does seeing her hurt you, too?" Of course it does. He wishes it was me that was pregnant.

"No. Seeing her doesn't hurt me. Seeing her hurt you, that hurts me."

Katie jogs over. "Mom, want me to come with you?"

"I'll be right back. I promise."

I want to sit in the dirt and cry at the concern I see on her face. "The game will be over soon anyway, Mom." She knows about the first miscarriage since I was in my fourth month. She doesn't even know about the second one because it was early in the pregnancy and...

"You don't have to come back," she says.

"It will only take me ten minutes..." Ten minutes to get coffee Michael probably doesn't even want—and to get control of myself. I fake a smile and wave over my shoulder as I take his keys and practically run to the parking lot.

Chapter Ten

I watch Katie run up the front stairs to Emily's house, pathetically grateful when she turns around to wave bye. With that morsel of affection, I head home after a very long day.

I remember once on vacation I dropped my digital camera and it would only let me take thirty-seven pictures. So every time I wanted to take one, I had to delete a picture. That's what life feels like right now. If I want to enjoy Katie at fourteen, I have to let go of Katie at two.

With Katie sleeping over at Emily's and Michael DJ-ing a wedding, I realize I have the night completely to myself. A glass of wine. A long, hot, uninterrupted bath. Can the night get any better?

A movie. I look over my shoulder and make a sharp right. I can get that shark movie about the couple who went scuba diving and got left alone out in the ocean. Or better yet, an oldie but goodie like *Thelma and Louise*.

I stop at the next light, stretching my neck, and that's when I see it. Across the street, in a small lot.

A black, convertible VW bug.

Thank heavens I am stopped at a light because a memory from long ago washes over me. I am eight years old, crammed on a school bus with twenty other kids, staring out the rectangular window the bus driver won't let us open. A woman, probably in her twenties, drives by in a black convertible bug. My friend punches me in the arm... "Punch buggy black, no punch back."

"That's a game for babies," I say. "That's the car I'm going to have when I grow up."

And there it is.

And here I am. All grown up, driving what is essentially a sporty station wagon. A car that makes sense. Makes it easy to lug stuff back and forth to the studio. It has five seat belts to take Katie's friends to the beach.

I think I hear Flat Julia suck in her breath as if she, too, recognizes the coolest car in the whole world. With a will of their own, my hands turn the steering wheel. The next thing I know, I have pulled into the used car lot that I have driven by for years and barely noticed.

I park beside the car, leave my keys on the dash, and drag my huge pocketbook with me.

"Quite a car, isn't she?" says the sales guy who suddenly appears out of nowhere. "She's got low mileage."

I check the odometer. Sixty thousand miles.

Ten thousand more than my car has.

"And she's only seven years old."

Two years older than my car.

"Want to take her for a test drive?"

I know I am supposed to play it cool, but I am beyond cool. "Hell, yeah!"

"Why don't you sit in it and get a feel while I go get the keys. And I need to make a copy of your license."

I hand it to him quickly, anxious for him to be gone. I want to be alone with the car.

My car.

As soon as he leaves, Flat Julia pipes up. "But what about all the recital props?"

I should have left her in the station wagon. "We can use Michael's truck."

"What about Katie's friends?"

Since when is Flat Julia the sensible one? "She'll have to pick and choose." I push a button and the roof is gone. I am not a Mom. Not a business owner. I am free!

"I want to trade cars," I say as soon as the salesman comes back.

"The blue book value on your car probably won't cover it. I'd say you'd need another thousand."

"Dollars? You want me to give you my newer car, with fewer miles, **and** a thousand dollars?"

"Hey, this is a convertible."

Like I didn't notice. "Yeah, but we live in New England. Surely there can't be much demand for a convertible."

"It's that time of year," he says, looking up at the blue sky.

It is clearly time to walk away. Time to play tough. Time to let him know I don't need this car.

"How about my car and five hundred dollars?" I offer.

He reaches his hand out and we shake. "Deal."

In no time, I fill out the paperwork, grab everything from the glove box and the trunk of my car, and give him a check.

I tuck Flat Julia on the dash, in the corner of the speedometer, and I swear she winks at me as I drive off in my new car!

I eat ice cream.... watch a movie On Demand... and every five minutes go to the window to make sure my car is really there.

And it is.

Right in my driveway. Parked like a sleeping little Herbie, just waiting for a signal from me that it is time to wake up, start our engine, and go off to find an adventure.

A little after midnight, Michael comes home. I happen to be by the window and see him take a peek. My car is utterly irresistible. And owning it, I feel irresistible.

He comes up the basement stairs and I meet him in the kitchen. "Who's here?" he whispers.

"Are you worried I have a hunk hiding in the bathroom?" I tease, my adrenaline still running high.

He laughs and kisses me. "Where's your car?"

"It's in the driveway," I say like the cat who not only ate the cream, but bathed in it as well.

He looks at me for a minute. "Jesus, Julia, she doesn't even have her learner's permit."

I shake my head. "It's not for Katie," I say. "It's mine."

"You? Miss Conservative, gotta-save-for-Katie's-college anytime I say let's go on a vacation even though I offer to pay for everything... you bought a second car?" He looks out the window, as if he has to convince himself its real. "You spent Eva's money on a car? A used car?"

"Not much of it. Only a couple hundred dollars."

"That car only cost you two hundred dollars?"

"Well, that," I say, thinking I can make an argument that five is a couple. "And my car."

"This isn't a second car for you?" He obviously thought my station wagon is in the garage.

"Nope," I say, so proud of myself. "I traded mine in and got this one."

"You traded in your safe, reliable, of-this-decade car, for that old piece of—"

"Heaven," I say, finishing the sentence for him. "Your girlfriend is pretty crazy, don'cha think?" This is way better than having a guy hiding in the bathroom. Michael is probably going to be so turned on he would try to take me right here in the kitchen. Or maybe I'd suggest we go out to the car and fool around... Katie is gone for the night... and after all, I am a wild woman.

"This is going to be your car all year?"

I nod.

"Do you know how it handles in the snow? Did you go online and check it out?"

"Well, if by "check it out" you mean did I just pull into the lot in one car and leave in another, then yes, I checked it out."

"That's not how you buy a car."

"Apparently, it is how I buy a car." Maybe it isn't the smartest way to buy a car, but shouldn't I get a few points for cool? For spontaneous? For listening to my nine-year-old voice?

"Seems crazy to me," he says. It is clear he doesn't mean crazy in the good, spontaneous, wild way.

"When winter comes and you're wanting to take the truck, it's going to cost you an arm and a leg to fill it up."

"My new car gets great gas mileage," I say, not sure if I am defending the car—or myself.

He raises an eyebrow.

"Fine," I admit. "I don't have any idea what kind of mileage it gets. And I don't care." Shit. Even I know that the price of gas is something to worry about, but I'm certainly not going to let him see me sweat.

"Whatever makes you happy," he says. He gets a glass of water and says he's going to bed.

I stand there and watch him walk upstairs. That is it... no congratulations... no can I have a ride?

I hear the toilet flush upstairs.

"Well, mister" I say, knowing I am drowned out by plumbing, "You can just forget about fooling around in my new car, or anywhere else, tonight!"

Chapter Eleven

I wake up early, one eye peeking out the window to check the weather. Please let it be sunny. Please let it be sunny.

I can't remember the last time I was excited to wake up or the last time I went to bed praying for Mother Nature to go along with my plans for an exciting day.

And like a good mother, she comes through.

I shower, grab a protein bar, and run out the door, my hair still wet. A convertible is the best blow dryer a girl could hope for.

Driving down the roads I have driven a million times, practically in my sleep, feels different without a roof. I am soaking up Vitamin D. I turn into the Dunkin Donuts drive-thru and pull up to the window. Maybe it's only my imagination, but I swear the three teenage girls working inside are looking at me in my car, hoping to grow up and be just like me—the kind of woman who owns a convertible because everyone knows "convertible" is synonymous with freedom, adventure, and nonconformity.

Not that any of those words are true about me.

Just the idea that someone is thinking any of those things about me feels like the wind is whispering that they are all possible.

Now that I have my coffee, a nice little confidence boost, and my convertible—the three C's I will never again live without—I decide to drive into the city and surprise Eva. After all, she's the one who gave me the ten thousand dollars to spend on myself.

And I know she will love what I am doing. Hiring someone to help me at the studio for the summer is brilliant. And buying this car is like a straight shot of Zoloft.

Although Eva is technically my aunt, she's more like a fairy godmother. She was a change-of-life baby for my grandparents, so she's ten years younger than my mother and exactly ten years older than me. Sometimes it feels like a tug of war between me and my mother. I always think I'm winning, but Eva has a way of making me feel like I'm the most important person in the whole world, so for all I know, my mother thinks the same thing.

The wind on the highway whips my hair into a frenzy, strands become a weapon of mass destruction to my vision. I reach into my purse and find a scrunchie, pulling my hair into a ponytail as well as I can.

I find a great parking space on the same side of the building as Eva's condo so she'll be able to see my car from her window. I stand there for a minute, fingering the key fob which has an automatic locking system. Am I supposed to lock a convertible? I lean in and put my CDs into the glove box, deciding that will be the extent of my security system. I run down to the corner store for more coffee and warm, chocolate croissants.

Eva's doorman waves me in, and I take the elevator up to the sixth floor and knock on Eva's door. "Breakfast delivery," I call.

Eva opens the door and throws her arms around me. I am home.

"Surprise! I've got breakfast," I say, balancing coffee on either side of her. Eva's hugs are legendary in our family. None of us quite knows her secret, but we all agree… there is something special about her hugs.

"And a new car!" she says, surprising me.

"How do you know?"

"I was sitting on my balcony when this hot little mama pulled up."

"That's me!"

We go inside, put our coffees on the granite breakfast bar, and head straight to the window. "When did you get a convertible?" she asks.

I smile. She doesn't call it a plain old car. She calls it a convertible. Big difference. "I got it yesterday."

"I didn't know you were looking for new wheels."

Wheels? I have wheels? Maybe I'm even cooler than I think. "I wasn't. I dropped Katie off at her friend's house. I was driving home, and I saw it."

"And you just bought it, then and there?"

Eva, the coolest, most spontaneous woman I have ever known, sounds impressed. "I did!"

"Honey-child, that sounds like something I would do."

Best compliment ever.

"How does it feel to drive it?" she asks, opening a glass cabinet in the kitchen for mugs. No plastic cups for her. She takes out two mugs that she made. She took a pottery class a few years ago and designed a mug. It was in the shape of an hourglass that also resembles a woman's torso. I have my own set at home that she gave me, but for some reason, I keep them safely in the buffet. Eva would kill me if she knew I was saving them. Note to self—take the damn mugs out and use them.

I smile. "Driving that car, you believe there might really be an adventure right around the next turn in the road."

"I want a ride—"

Of course she does. Second note to self—next time I do something crazy like this, ask Eva to send the appropriate script to Michael. Then maybe I could get to the sex part of my plan and not be detoured by his sensibility.

"But Phillip is on his way over," Eva says. "Can you stay for a bit?"

I finally notice our reflection in the window. Eva has on a long, red satin Oriental robe, the kind most women don't own, never mind wear. A terry cloth towel is wrapped around her head.

"I'm conditioning my hair before Phillip comes over," she explains.

In the glass, I look like Medusa on speed. I turn away from the window—no sense risking turning myself to stone today—and head straight for the chocolate. "How do you manage to get a hairdresser who does house calls?" I ask, going into the cupboard for some small plates for the croissants. No matching dinner sets for Eva. I pull out two of the plates from her fortieth birthday party. She had invited us all to one of those make-it-yourself pottery places. I had painted my plate black like a record and wrote on top "Produced with Love," to which Katie had asked what I was making since she had never seen a record. Mine was on top. Katie's beach plate was right under mine. "I could be bleeding to death on the floor and a doctor wouldn't come to my house."

"Who says you can't have your hairdresser come to your house?"

"Oh, I don't know. Us mere mortals?"

"If that works for you, great. This works for me. My hairdresser wanted to learn salsa. I wanted my hair done. We do both the first Sunday of the month."

"In your living room?"

"Yup. He puts the color on, and I put the music on."

I sigh. "Have I mentioned I want to be you when I grow up?"

"So you can stay for a while?"

"I'm not picking Katie up until this afternoon. And I'm not talking to Michael, although he doesn't know it, so don't tell him."

We take our coffee and croissants out onto her balcony, overlooking the city and my pretty little car. "He didn't say what you wanted to hear?"

"Hell, no. When he saw the car, he got all practical on me. He didn't appreciate how spontaneous I am."

"You know you don't need him to appreciate you if you're doing it yourself."

"It's more fun together."

Eva gets up and stands behind my chaise lounge. "If I could get this elastic-thingy out, you could try my new conditioner. Phillip says it's the bomb, whatever that means."

I can feel her grimacing behind me. Eva had probably never worn a scrunchie, even in the eighties when they were in style.

"I think this thing has mated with your hair. It might have to be cut out."

"You want to cut up my last scrunchie? Possibly the last scrunchie in New England?"

"I can try to get it out..."

"Go ahead," I tease. "You can cut it."

"I'll be right back," she says.

Relaxed by chocolate, and coffee, and the sun, I close my eyes, still seeing my little black car behind my eyelids. Eva comes back, scissors in hand, and proceeds to cut the scrunchie holding my hair on top of my head. Then she rubs some coconut-avocado-paradise smelling cream on my hair. I feel like a baby having her mother tenderly wash her hair.

"If you promise to show Phillip some tap dancing, he might have time to do your hair this morning, too."

"Funny, I was just telling Charlotte about my short blonde hair. Remember?"

"Of course I remember. Your mother almost died when you came home with that bleached blonde hair. 'Shorter than a Marine's' she called it."

"I barely used a brush. Just my fingers, a blow dryer, and some gel and I was ready to go." I try to turn, but she starts massaging my scalp with her fingertips and I fall back in the chair. "Speaking of Charlotte, I proposed."

"Aren't you already involved?"

Leave it to Eva to only say that. "Remember the creep she was seeing?"

"The married one? I thought she broke that off."

"Yeah, well apparently, the bastard can't take rejection. Supposedly he divorced his wife, waited the three months Charlotte had said for him to take to heal, and he mailed her an engagement ring. Can you believe it? He mailed an engagement ring. It fell out of the box and I proposed to her myself."

Eva laughed. "Did she say yes?"

"To me? Or to him?"

"Either."

"For a second, I thought she was considering it. You should have seen her face. It was the last thing she expected from him. I told her she didn't owe him anything. And you know what she said?"

"She looked at me all serious, and said, 'Don't I owe it to myself?'"

"I'm sure as her friend you just want her to be happy."

"Well, yes. Of course. But she is happy. Right here. She doesn't need to be moving to North Carolina with a lousy cheater to be happy. I put together a great breakup package and I'm going to give it to her tonight when Katie goes to the movies."

"So tell me what else is going on in your life."

"Let's see. I bought the car. And I've put an ad in the paper for help this summer. Someone to get me computerized, paint the studio, and organize. If I find the right person, I'll pretty much have the summer off. Except for dance camp. But that's not until August." She is now combing the conditioner through my hair with a fine comb. If my hair could stand up and hug her, it would. "And Katie's going to Disney World over vacation with her friend's family."

"That's great for her. So what else?" I knew she was asking for more than details about my life. Eva never got sidetracked with details; she always wanted to talk to your heart.

"I had a dream last night."

"Hmm?"

"I was underwater, but it was okay because I knew I could hold my breath for a long time and I was enjoying floating without weight. But then the sign from the studio, the one hanging outside the building with the gold chain, was around my neck, and it was pulling me under. I knew at some point I'd need air, and I could see the light and the surface getting farther and farther away. It was like I was hanging and drowning at the same time."

"Sounds like some time off is exactly what you need."

"I'm just tired. I feel like I can't catch up to my own life. It's one step forward, two steps back. I'm tired of working so hard. Tired of being responsible all the time." *Tired of this life.*

"Maybe you're ready for a new life," she says as if she heard my thoughts.

"But I'm fixing things," I say, hating the whine I hear in my own voice.

"Maybe you don't need to fix. Maybe you need to start over."

That is easy for her to say. Easy for Charlotte to contemplate chucking it all and starting over. But I have a family. And no one has any idea how much that changes the whole game until they do it.

"Joseph Campbell says, 'You must give up the life you had planned in order to have the life that is waiting for you.'"

"I might give up stuff if I knew what I wanted. But give up things I used to love for what? For nothing? For something I like even less?"

"To find yourself."

"I just want to find the old me. This new and improved me, well, she kinda sucks."

"We get stuck with identities and forget ourselves. What titles would you give me?"

"Best aunt in the whole world."

Eva smiles. "What else?"

"Fabulous ballroom dancer. World traveler. Artist. You owned a book store for a while when I was little. Is it still there?"

Eva laughs. "I don't know," she says, refusing to be sidetracked. "You know what titles I give myself?"

"All of those. Plus a million more cool titles?"

"None. None of them. Although Best Aunt has a nice ring to it. I don't define myself by anything. So I'm not stuck. I can be what I want now. And then something else tomorrow. I pick up identities like clothes. Some I buy and wear for a while. Some I just buy and hang in my closet. An identity is as easy to toss as an old blouse."

I sigh, wishing it were that simple. "But some identities become printed on your soul."

Eva moves to the other chair and sits across from me. "I'm not saying it's easy. It takes practice. Believe me, I started accumulating titles very young, as we all do, long before we really have any idea who we are."

"How did you become such a free thinker? Most of us spend our lives hoping that for one second, we'll get a chance to step outside the box. You wouldn't know a line if it bit you in the ass."

"Because I played by the rules for the first twenty or so years of my life, too. Then life changed the rules on me. I'd been taught do the right thing, go to school, be smart, be sensible, and you'll be safe. Well, turns out I wasn't safe. None of us are safe. So you can play by the rules, thinking that life will return the favor. And it very well may. But it will be because that's what your life is meant to be. Not as a reward for being a 'good girl.'"

"When were you not safe? Life wouldn't dare go up against you."

"Oh, my darling, it did."

This is a side of Eva I've never seen. Serious. Somber.

"What happened?"

She looks at me for a minute, studying me. I imagine Eva suddenly standing up like Jack Nicholson—'You can't handle the truth!'"

"In college... " she starts.

"You went to college? I didn't know that." Am I interrupting because she's right? Maybe I don't want to know the truth. It looks scary.

"For a couple of years. I was accumulating titles like everyone else, adding them one at a time like a juggler adds a ball. Then the love of my life died."

"What?!"

"That was it. Every title that I had—student, good girl, daughter—that I thought defined me, that I clung to viciously and with ego and pride, they all fell away. My heart was broken and nothing else mattered. And I had no intention of moving on. I was the poor young girl who had lost the love of her life. I was the star of my own little drama, and I was going to stay that way."

"How come I don't know all of this?"

"I don't talk about it."

"I would have thought that I'd at least know."

"How would I have explained that the only man I ever really loved died without your thinking I was a victim? You'd be stuck like I was, in a trap, seeing poor me. You would use that to define me. I'd be the best aunt in the whole world who tragically lost the love of her life."

"Why are you telling me now?"

"Because maybe you can see that as much as it hurt—my heart being burned to ashes, as painful as it was—it was also the catalyst that set me free. So when I finally felt up to living again, I was going to do whatever the hell I pleased. I had played by the rules and I got hurt. So I learned: Playing by the rules doesn't keep you safe. I wasn't afraid anymore."

I had always wondered how someone as fabulous as Eva could be alone. I figured there was no man special enough for her. But there had been. "How did you get over it?"

"My friend Meg. She let me wallow for almost a year. She let me submerge myself in my pain. Everyone else wanted me to go back to school, to get on with my life. Meg seemed to know I was in the fire and I had to stay there until I was cooked. It was the best gift I've ever been given. Because then I came out of it. I mean, really healed, not just pretend heal, pull-up-your-bootstraps-and-move-on heal. And if I wasn't going to be the poor me that lost the love of my life, then there wasn't any identity that could stick to me or define me. I try things on—careers, lifestyles, places to live—like outfits. I don't get attached to them. I don't identify myself by them."

She holds my hands in hers. "You're the one that has built the box, honey, that you feel so closed in by. What titles are you holding onto? That you are allowing to define and limit you?"

"Single mother. Dancer."

"I'm surprised single mother is still there. Katie's dad is in the picture and you're living with Michael. And truth be told, you're not a dancer now either. You're not consumed by it. Sounds like you just tolerate it now."

"So what am I?"

"You can be anything you want to be."

"What if all I feel is lost?"

"Then you've got to do as the butterfly does."

"Fly away?"

"A caterpillar doesn't just go to sleep in the cocoon and wake up with wings. It literally dissolves. If you cut open the cocoon, it's a liquid goop of nothing. Not caterpillar. Certainly not butterfly. Just goop."

"You want me to turn myself into goop?" Playing dumb is easier than admitting I already feel like some melted, messy, dirty version of my old self.

"The caterpillar doesn't make it out alive. That messy goop, the DNA in those cells, somehow knows how to rebuild itself into something else." She squeezes my hands, and I want to throw myself at her and disappear into one of her hugs.

"I was a caterpillar, walking through life, doing what I was supposed to. And don't get me wrong, I was happy. Happy enough, anyway. And if life hadn't blown me up, I'd still be a caterpillar."

The doorbell rang.

"And probably getting my hair done in a salon, at an inconvenient time."

"Saved by the bell," I say to her. "That robe is much too pretty for me to get my goop all over it anyway."

"If you were happy as a caterpillar, I would love you as a caterpillar forever."

I try to smile. "Can you love indiscriminate goop?"

She kisses me on the forehead and looks into my eyes. "I loved you when you were a caterpillar, and I love you now even more as goop. And I promise I'll love you when you get your wings under you again, too."

"Can you love me enough for both of us?" I whisper. "Just for a little while?"

She nods and I am almost ashamed how good it feels to know someone loves me, in spite of my being a mess.

"Anyone home?" a voice calls from inside.

Eva smiles, still holding my hand. "We're on the porch."

Phillip poses in the door frame. His jeans are ripped so perfectly I want to get up and study them. In high school I spent hours with a brillo pad trying to achieve that cool, distressed look. There's no doubt he paid through the nose for those jeans. And speaking of noses, he has a sparkling diamond nose ring in his. It should be over the top but it actually suits him.

He takes a deep breath, making sure he has our full attention. "The door was open and we've got a serious problem," he says. "More serious than five years ago when you forced me to put that awful champagne blonde on you. I told you we needed to stick to blue-based colors, but you insisted." He shudders and holds up a flyer of a man that looks like a Greek God. "This," Phillip says, "is the man I am supposed to have coaching me this week."

"Marco is an incredible dancer," Eva says. "What's the problem?"

Phillip scratches his head. "I thought you knew," he says flamboyantly, "but apparently you need it spelled out for you. I'm gay."

"You've had coaching with men before," Eva says.

"Yeah. With sixty-year-old, bald guys. This guy is young. And he's hot."

"He's almost forty," Eva says, "and you can't hold his hotness against him."

Phillip poses dramatically, his hands on his hips. "That's the problem, honey," he says with a Mae West accent. "I want to hold his hotness against me a little too much."

I lift the picture. "I have to agree. He's hot. Hotter than hot. Hotter than this city has seen since..."

"Yes," Eva says patiently, "Marco is attractive."

"I'm attractive," I say. "Calling him attractive is almost an insult." When Phillip looks me up and down skeptically, I blush. "On a good day," I say, "with a bit of effort, I can be attractive."

Phillip simply raises one very skeptical eyebrow.

"Phillip, you remember my niece, Julia."

"Nice to see you again," he says. We met once a long time ago, but I doubt he remembers.

"All I can say is," he says dramatically, helping himself to a croissant, "I can't promise to control myself."

I study the picture for a moment. "I don't think you should control yourself. A man walks around looking like this, well, then he deserves to have people throw themselves all over him. I don't know whose team he plays for..."

Eva grabs the picture out of my hand. "I can't believe you two! Judging someone from a picture. And I hate to tell you both," she says with a sultry grin, "but that picture ain't doing him justice. In person, you find out his soul is even prettier than his face."

Phillip and I gasp at the same time.

"That's it. Cancel my lesson," Phillip says, taking another pastry. How the hell does he get into those teeny tiny jeans?

"You've been after me to bring in good male coaches."

"Yeah. To teach me how to be a good leader. And this guy certainly is all male. I wouldn't mind being this man's lady, if you know what I mean, but I am not dancing with him by myself. And my partner's out of town, so we'll just have to cancel."

"Julia could partner with you on the lesson."

We both look at her. "Huh?"

"Julia could dance with you. She's a professional dancer. Owns her own studio.

"I'm a tapper," I remind her.

"I taught you to waltz before you learned to walk. And it's only because of the pretty shoes that made noise that you decided to seriously study tap."

"I picked shoes over dancing with men who look like this?"

Eva shrugs her shoulders.

I look at her. "Why don't you dance with him?"

"I think you need him right now more than I do," she says.

Phillip looks me up and down again, wincing when he gets to my head. "I was planning on working on tango," he says. "Do you know the tango?"

Eva answers for me. "Tango is her best dance."

"She doesn't look like a tango dancer," he says suspiciously.

"You could do her hair this morning and then we could show her your routine."

Two can play the insult game. "I'm not going to let some weekend warrior hairdresser cut my hair." Of course, I know he's a great hair stylist if Eva likes him, but this back and forth banter is rather fun.

"I'm a lover, and a tango-er, honey, not a warrior. And there's nothing weekend about me. I own the Solstice Salon on Newbury Street. Maybe you've heard of it?"

Shit! I know Eva would have only the best, but Solstice Salon? It is the poshest salon in the city. I've read about it, driven by it, and even dreamt about going there, but there is always a month's wait, and I can never wait that long. At least that's what I tell myself, ignoring the little detail that I could never afford it.

He stares at me. "Are you as good as Eva says you are?"

"Better."

He snaps his fingers again. "You dance with me," he says, "and I'll make you beautiful."

I spin around and do a corte, the only tango step I remember. "You make me beautiful, and I'll dance you like you've never been danced before."

He takes me into dance position and does a quick little pivot around the granite breakfast bar. Without thinking, I switch our positions and dip him. He let out a very unmasculine yelp!

"She was thinking short," Eva says.

He stands up and pushes me onto one of the barstools, feeling my hair this way and that. "If you go short, and stick with your natural color, you'll look like a soccer mom. And I'm sorry, honey, but I don't do soccer moms."

"I'm guessing you don't 'do' any moms."

He gives me a quick high five then gets back to business. "What if we go really short and give her a wow color?" he asks Eva.

"I'm too old for platinum," I say, starting to get nervous. Isn't it daring enough that I am going to cut off most of my hair? Am I ready for wow color, too?

"Who says you're too old?" Eva asks.

"I do," Phillip and I say in chorus.

Phillip steps back and stands beside Eva, both of them staring at me as if I am not there. Only my head, and that is only there because there is hair growing out of it.

"We could go very dark," Phillip says. "It could be dramatic with her light skin."

"Black?" I cry. "I'll look like Count Dracula in drag."

"Count Dracula in drag would be a woman, dummy."

"Well, I'd look like Countess Dracula in drag," I say. I'm not sure they get it, so I explain, "I'll look like a guy."

"Then there's only one thing left to do," he says simply.

Eva jumps up and down, clapping her hands. "Red!" they say in stereo.

Chapter Twelve

I arrive at Emily's house to pick up Katie. Tina, Emily's mom, is at the front door of her split level house. "Someone's mom is here," she says. I see Katie and two of her friends come up the stairs and glance out. They both say "Not mine," and turn away, continuing up the stairs.

I beep again and wave. "Katie!"

Tina opens the screen door. "Is that...?"

Katie looks out again. "Mom?"

Tina walks down the front stairs in her bare feet, her hands shielding her eyes from the bright sun. "Julia?" she says. I hear the question in her voice and I swear I see a gleam of respect in her eye as she comes closer. "Is that you?"

She's standing right next to my car, leaning on my door. I can't get out, so I just grin up at her.

"Your hair!"

I reach up and stroke the back of my bare neck. "I needed a change," I say.

"You look fabulous."

Emily has followed her mom out, Katie on her heels. "Mrs. Stone, this is the coolest car ever! Mom, can we get one?"

Tina puts her arm around Emily's shoulders. "Yeah, we'll just go out this afternoon and pick up some milk... and a new car."

I know what she means... that it isn't that easy. And yet it is. When do we stop thinking things will be easy? When we find out that nothing is easy—even getting milk. Organic? Two percent?

99

Whole? And all the experts have opinions and facts to back them up, until it changes the next week. When do we lose the ability to make our own decisions?

So far, Katie hasn't said anything, but she certainly doesn't look as impressed as the Brown family.

"And your hair!" Emily says. "Short hair is so in style right now." Funny, she and her mom probably like my new hair for very different reasons. Emily thinks it is cool, and Tina is trying to remember why she hasn't had a new hairstyle in thirteen years. Emily and her sisters are why. They are the ones who need the attention. They need new clothes every year because they outgrow them constantly. So it is easier, and logical, and somehow right that we continue to wear what we have. We don't need new clothes for the school year. We don't need new clothes to prove that we are cool. And if last year's clothes don't fit, we don't need new clothes. We need a diet. And if we absolutely have to, we buy the bigger size in the dark, like drug addicts buy their stash, on the sly, with lots of guilt.

I can't help myself. I look at Katie. "Do you like our new car?" *Or my short, red hair?*

"Will you let me drive it?"

What? She only likes it if she can drive it? Holding her approval hostage? "We'll see."

"And your hair, Mom. You cut it all off."

Nothing like stating the obvious. If that's her reaction, God knows what Michael's will be. Maybe I won't go home until it grows a bit. "I was at Eva's this morning, and her stylist from Solstice Salon..."

"No wonder you look so chic," Tina says. "Why don't you help Katie get her stuff," Tina says to the girls and they walk off.

"I can't tell if Katie likes my new car or not," I say, not wanting to admit she is raining on my parade.

"I can't tell if Emily likes me half the time," Tina says, only half-joking. "You're raising the bar."

I'm raising the bar? It sounds like a bad thing for Katie, but

I can't help the rush of pleasure that I'm raising anything.

"Katie is the one who is supposed to be rebelling and growing right now. She's the one who is supposed to do wild and crazy things. And you're raising the bar for her."

"Why does that have an ominous sound, like, 'I'll be sorry'?"

"Hey, if you're ever really sorry, you can park that baby in my driveway, you know, just until things cool over. And make sure you leave the keys over the visor, in case I have to move it. Or get in it one day and run away to Key West."

Katie comes out with her bags and throws them in the back seat. She sits in the passenger seat, leaning against the door. Sulking. "You acted like we couldn't afford an airline ticket for me to go to Florida, and here you go buying a new car," she says as I back out of the driveway.

Silly me. Of course my buying a new car and cutting my hair is all about her. "So if I have X amount of money, then I should use it for you to go to Florida first, and then if I have anything left, I can buy a car?"

"You don't need a car," she says.

"And you don't need to go to Florida."

"You had a perfectly good car."

"And you have a perfectly good home you can stay at and never have to leave." Although at the moment, that seems more like punishment to me than to her.

I take a deep breath and squeeze the steering wheel. Teenagers are supposed to be self-absorbed, I remind myself. It's in their DNA. And it fits the whole process of evolution perfectly. There is no way a mother would be able to survive separation from her baby except in fifteen minute increments. But then cute baby turns into something completely unrecognizable, something that obliterates your cute little baby—a teenager. The whole point of adolescence is to prepare you for the fact that your little bird is going to fly the coop. The teen years actually make you want to push them out.

"If Michael hadn't given me his miles, I probably wouldn't be able to go.

How the hell did Katie and Michael end up on the same team... aligned against me?

Men are as clueless, as selfish, and as unsupportive as a teenager. And there's no hope of sending them off to college. "If you think the reason you are going is because Michael gave you his miles, you're sadly mistaken. You're going because I want you to have a great vacation."

"Sorry, Mom. It's just embarrassing not to know your own mother when she comes to pick you up." She sits up a little straighter. "If you can cut off all your hair, can I get my bellybutton pierced?"

I think about letting go of the steering wheel and choking her until neither one of us can see, but then I notice the little minx has a twinkle in her eye. She's teasing me.

Keeping up with her mood changes is draining. I am getting better at it, knowing no matter how bad the mood, it won't last. But tiptoeing gets tiring. Why doesn't anyone tiptoe around me? Eva is right. I like the sound of my tap shoes clicking as I walk. How did I go from someone who liked making noise to someone who tiptoed constantly?

"If you're going to be the coolest Mom around..."

I'm the coolest Mom around? We are going to hit a tree... not because I'm choking her, but because I think I'm going to cry.

"...then I should get my bellybutton pierced."

I go back to clenching the wheel. Teenagers should come with conversation referees. One minute it is Katie my sweetie-pie swinging her racket of conversation, then it is Katie the Witch's turn to hit the ball. It is hard to keep up with who's talking out of Katie's body. Maybe I'll start playing the game, too.

"Should I get my belly button pierced, too?" I ask.

"God, no, Mom. That's gross. You're like forty-something."

Thirty-eight isn't forty-something, but I bite my tongue. "At least we agree on something," I say. "Belly button rings are gross."

"I'll take that as a no." She thinks for a minute. "A tattoo?"

"Should I get a tattoo?" I ask.

She looks about ready to say no, but instead she asks, "What would you get?"

"Your name," I say, flexing my arm, "on my bulging bicep?"

Katie giggles, her head thrown back, her hair blowing in the breeze. God, I love her. Maybe I'm starting to get the hang of this teenage chameleon thing. Nice for two minutes. Nasty for two. Then she'll settle into normal for eight minutes. Then the whole cycle starts over. So the trick is like trying to join in on an already swinging jump rope. It's all about timing.

"Forget the tattoo. How about I get the top of my ear pierced?"

"What is this? I get something, you get something?"

"Why not?" she asks with such honesty that I can't really find fault. Except I do wonder why this game doesn't apply when she gets something. When I give her a ride? When I give her money?

"C'mon, Mom. A little gold hoop at the top of my ear, really little."

"I don't know..."

"With your new short hair, it would look really good on you."

Was she suggesting...?

"We could do it together."

I try to play it cool. I really do. Because winning is half the fun for her, so I can't give in too easy. "I don't know, Katie..."

"C'mon, Mom. We can do it together. Mother-daughter bonding. And we'll always think of each other when we touch it. When I go off to college..."

I know I'm being wrapped around her little finger and I don't care. "Maybe. When softball is over."

She reaches up and gives me a high five. I try to pretend I haven't given in, but we both know I have. How can I resist mother-daughter bonding? I look up at the sky, thanking heaven that this brilliant, beautiful, self-absorbed child is all mine.

Chapter Thirteen

While I am waiting for the Chinese food that I ordered to take over to Charlotte's, I check my voice mail. I have three messages:

First message: "Hi Julia. This is Toby's mom. I saw your ad posted on the bulletin board at the studio. As you might remember, I'm an attorney in Boston. I've been thinking that while Toby is young, now might be a good time for me to do something other than law, closer to home. I've got a proposition for you. Call me back and hopefully we can set up a time to talk."

Holy moly! Someone's calling about the job.

Message Two: "My name is Lily and I'm calling about the summer position listed on Craigslist. Here's my number so you can call me back. Thanks."

Double Holy moly! Two people are calling about the joSb! I want to do a jig in the lobby of the Lilac Garden.

Message Three: "Hi, Julia. This is Lucy Thompson, your old neighbor. I was walking by your condo yesterday, and I noticed the door was ajar. I knocked to see if anything was wrong, and it was completely empty. I never saw a moving truck, and I haven't seen your tenant in a couple of weeks now. You probably know this, but I couldn't stop thinking about it last night. I figured it's better to be safe than sorry."

Damn! Damn! Damn! Triple damn. Seems my tenant, who owes for the last three months, is MIA!

The hostess signals that my food is ready, and I grab the bag and go out to my car. "Okay, God," I begin to negotiate. Driving down the highway at seventy miles an hour in the convertible with nothing between me and the sky, I feel like I have a direct line to God. "It seems no matter how much I try to clear my plate, the minute, the second it looks like I might actually get a moment to take a deep breath, you heap something else on it. You don't even wait to see if either of these women is going to work out so that I can have a bit of time off. It's like you're up there, standing behind the proverbial fan. Oh, looks like Julia *might* be getting some help at the studio. Now's a perfect time to have her tenant run off."

I pull up to Charlotte's, without a response from you-know-who, and sit in the car for a moment. One thing at a time. Tonight is about Charlotte. I get out of my car and grab the food and the breakup package I made for her. I can't wait to show her my new hair. And my new car!

The fortune cookies that are balanced on top of the paper bag start rolling around. I try to dance under it, like a juggler balancing a stack of plates. A single cookie falls and with my next step I hear it crunch into a million pieces under my foot. The good news is I save the remaining cookies. The bad news is a single white worm of a fortune mocks me from beneath the edge of my dirty Ked sneaker. I know this fortune is meant for me.

I put my packages on the hood of the car and pick up the murdered fortune from the cookie debris. Maybe God talks through fortune cookies.

"Your life is _____."

Literally. That's what it says. "Your life is..." Blank. Fill in the blank. Empty space. Clearly I'm in the thick of a midlife crisis, thinking God is talking through Chinese cookies, and that's the best I can get? My life is one big blank? I don't need a cookie, or God, to tell me that.

I grind the rest of the cookie into dust for good measure and walk up the path to Charlotte's condo. The door is open and

Charlotte has music playing. Fun music. I think it's the Pointer Sisters' "I'm So Excited."

I stand like a statue at Charlotte's open front door, the screen door between us, my breakup package heavy in my arms. She is packing. And not just a suitcase—she is packing boxes. "Oh. My. God. You're going."

Charlotte smiles. Not her normal smile. Not her happy smile, or her sad smile, but a forced smile. I can't breathe. It is the first time in our friendship that we are faking it.

"Looks like I'm getting my HEA," Charlotte says, using my term. Happily Ever After is my term!

"Since when have you wanted HEA?" I ask, still standing at the door. I can't move forward. And we are talking, so I can't turn around, drive home, and pretend I don't know what she is doing.

"We all want it in our own way. Sometimes when it shows up, it doesn't look like we thought it would," she says.

"You can't just leave," I say.

"I can," she says softly, as if she is afraid to say those words to me. As if she knows those two simple words may knock me off my axis.

"No you can't. You can't just get up and leave your life. What about your condo?"

"I'll lock it."

"What about your business?"

"Margi's going to come on full-time and be my manager. Her youngest is going into high school this year and she's been after me for more responsibility."

I shift from foot to foot. "What about the doll business we are starting?"

"I put everything I have in a box."

"You're just going to take them? All our work? It was my idea to begin with." Here was something tangible that she was taking from me. Something I could fight for.

"Of course I'm not going to just take them," she says, going into the closet and pulling out a box. "We can still do it, if we want. We can keep shopping. Send each other pictures of what we get."

"Sure, we'll just leave the dolls naked until we can get together."

"Julia," she says softly, "there aren't any completed dolls yet. You still have to make them."

"Right," I say, finally going inside. I drop her breakup package on the floor and open the box of dissembled doll limbs. Arms and legs and torsos all reaching out for completion. "It's my fault we haven't gotten any further."

"I'm not saying it's anyone's fault," she says.

"The needle on my sewing machine broke. I told you I ordered a special needle." So what if I haven't told her it came in. Weeks ago.

"There's no rush."

Of course there is. She's moving far away. "What about your friends?" *What about me?* A volcano of bubbling emotion presses on my chest.

"My cell number will be the same. It will work in North Carolina. And there's e-mail. And visits."

"I don't want to visit you once a year. I want to visit you every Monday like I do now."

She smiles, a real smile, a sad smile. "I will miss our Monday mornings, too."

"I don't understand. I thought you hadn't talked to him—"

"I haven't."

I hold the box tight to my chest. "You haven't talked to this man in almost a year," I say, wondering if I believe her. "You haven't seen him. How do you know you still love him?"

"You don't just stop loving a person."

No, I thought. A smart person doesn't start loving someone who isn't available. That was Charlotte's first mistake. Apparently not her last. I wonder why I can hear the whistle blowing, warning that the train is coming, and driving across the tracks now means certain death. How come Charlotte can't hear the warning bells that are ringing loud enough to wake the dead?

"A year ago, I told him if he got divorced," Charlotte says, "not to call me for three months. To give him time to adjust."

"Three months isn't long enough to get over your parakeet dying, never mind a divorce," I say.

Charlotte keeps wrapping plates and putting them in a box. "He wants to buy a gym out there for me."

"Why can't Ken move here?" I ask.

"He's wants to stay near his kids. And you know me, I like adventure."

"You just had an adventure at the dude ranch."

"Vacation is fun, but it isn't a life adventure. Moving to North Carolina, kinda spur of the moment, that's a pretty good adventure."

"You say adventure, I say..." *Mistake.* "Why not take it slow? Go visit him?"

"He made his big move; he left his wife. We never thought he'd do that."

"So because he made a grand gesture, you have to make a big move?"

"Julia, people move all the time."

"No, they don't. Well, they do, but they plan it. They get a promotion, or..."

"Is that what's bothering you? My reason? Would a new job be a good enough reason for me to move, according to you?" She rips off a long piece of tape and seals another box. "Would you be pacing my condo like a caged tiger if I was moving for a job, or would you be helping me pack?"

The breakup gift basket is cutting off the circulation in my arm. "You don't owe him anything," I say.

"I owe it to myself."

"I think moving to be with a man who cheated..."

"You always held that against him."

"Well, he did cheat." Shouldn't I hold that against him?

"But he didn't cheat alone. I was a cheater, too. So why aren't you mad at me?"

"Because..."

"Because I'm your friend?"

"Because you're not the one who is married. He is. Was. Whatever. Now he wants to marry you."

Charlotte grabs a handful of silverware, wrapping the forks with the spoons and the knives in newspaper. "Why are you trying to talk me out of this?"

I bite my tongue, wanting to bite it off and lash her with it at the same time.

"Tell me!"

"He's a lousy, two-timing bastard who only wants you because you dumped him. As soon as you get settled out there, he's going to cheat on you."

"What gives you the right to judge him? Or me?" She asks, standing up and facing me. "How would you like it?"

"Go ahead."

"Fine," she says. "You're miserable. You're unhappy. You're spinning your wheels around and digging yourself deeper and deeper into your life. I'm starting to think it's just so you can be unhappy. And the more the world tells you you've got it all, the man and the kid and the job, the more you buy into it, knowing with all your heart that it's not working for you. I'm starting to think you want to be unhappy. You're only happy when you're unhappy."

"This isn't about me."

"You're damn right it isn't," she says, crossing her arms.

"I think you're making a mistake."

"So I should just sit around and not get what I want because that would make you happy?"

"I want <u>you</u> to be happy!" I say.

"But not this way, right? Because I didn't play by the rules."

"I don't want to see you get hurt. You deserve better."

"Is it really about me? Or is this about you? You played by the rules and you hate your HEA. So the thought that I could find mine, after doing everything wrong, makes you crazy." She slams one box on top of another. "Goes against everything you think you know. Makes you wonder why you ever bothered playing by the rules."

"I don't think you'll be happy with him. Once a cheater, always a cheater." There, I've said it.

"And I don't think you'll be happy until you get off your ass, but I've been your friend whether you get up or keep whining about the same things you've whined about for the past two years. Even though I know you don't agree with what I'm doing, I need you."

I want to put the box down and go to her, but I can't. I can't move. "I hate him! He doesn't deserve you."

"How do you know? You've never met him."

"Exactly. I'm your best friend and he's never even met me. That tells me he's not into you, not into your life, what is good for you. He's just taking care of himself."

"Maybe that's why you don't like him," she says softly.

"Because he's selfish?"

"No. Because he's going after what he wants. And so am I. And that's bugging the shit out of you. Because you're not. You are jealous."

"Oh, I'm really jealous you're going to be with a cheater."

"Because you and Michael haven't cheated on each other, as far as you know anyway, that's your claim to happiness? That you've subscribed to monogamy? How's that working out for you?" Charlotte throws some of the wrapped silverware into a box. Glass shatters. "I think Michael's a great guy. And I think he's good for you. But you won't let him. It's like you don't want him to be good for you. I almost wouldn't blame him if he did cheat on you."

I gasp. "Then I guess it's a good thing you're moving." I turn and walk away, carrying a box of broken doll parts that I'm afraid will never be made whole.

Chapter Fourteen

I sit in Madelyn's office, Charlotte's breakup package held firmly on my lap, a personal talisman of what a good friend I am.

"Remember, I told you about my friend Charlotte?"

Madelyn nods, her ever-present pad of paper resting on her lap.

"She had been seeing this married guy, but she broke up with him a while back. This week he had the nerve to send her an engagement ring in the mail. Even though he's a jerk, I figured she'd be upset, so last night I went over to give her the breakup package I put together." I open the box and pull out the top item. "First, we have the "Bridget Jones' Diary II" DVD. We watched the first one when she dumped Ken. If I could have rented the New Year's Eve ball from Times Square to celebrate the occasion I would have. If I could have had him standing under it when it dropped, much quicker than usual, right onto his head..." I reach in and pull out two bags. "Pretzels and Rollos. I like pretzels and she likes Rollos," I explain. "You know the Reese's Peanut Butter Cup commercials where a person with peanut butter and a person with chocolate bump into each other? They're better together. That's us. And this is our snack." I sigh. I wouldn't have to explain any of these things to Charlotte.

I pull out the next thing. "And black stationary to write Ken a scathing note for when she sends the ring back." I smile. "I was going to suggest sending it back uninsured." I reach into the box again, pulling out some papers. "And if she's ready to date again, I went on Match.com and printed some pictures and bios of some very interesting, unmarried—"

"As far as you know," ET interjects.

I ignore her comment. "UN-married," I repeat, "local guys." I pull out the blow-up boyfriend. "You water him and he grows." I glance around the closed office. I hold up the flap of the box, just letting her peek at the last item. "I even found a joint in the bottom of my old jewelry box. It's probably not any good, but I thought it would make her laugh anyway."

Tink smiles. "Well, it may not be any good, but it's still illegal."

Is she required by law to report me? "I'll throw it away," I offer.

"Not here you won't."

There's a thought. I could plant the ancient doobie in her office for the "They're not married—as far as you know" crack. "You know... the best way to get rid of evidence..."

"Smoke it," we say in harmony.

"It probably wouldn't get us high," she says laughing, "but we'd still get the munchies. And I just started working out again, so I can't chance it. Sorry," she says—like that's her only reason. "You can go into my private bathroom and flush it."

I put Charlotte's things back into her box, feeling like I am packing up the home of a recently deceased relative. I go into her bathroom and look at the water in the toilet bowl and the single joint in my hand. I stick it in my pocket and flush the toilet.

"Since you brought your care package here," she says when I come back, "I'm guessing you didn't give it to Charlotte."

"No. You're not going to believe what she was doing when I got there."

"Growing fresh marijuana?"

"This isn't funny. She was packing. She's going to move to North Carolina to be with him. She promoted her employee to manager, she's closing up her condo..." I stutter, my mouth not

able to keep up with all the words ricocheting around in my head.

"She even packed up our doll stuff, pretending we could still start a business while we are living in different states."

"Are you mad your business partner is abandoning you? Or madder at yourself because you won't do it alone?"

I throw my hands up in the air. "You're right. Silly me. I should be able to own a dance studio, be a landlord without a tenant, a mom, a girlfriend, and then on the twenty-ninth hour of the day, start another business, all without sleeping. Who needs sleep? I'll be the poster child of the modern woman."

"You'll be the poster child of Prozac."

We stare at each other. It feels like a standoff.

"Let's talk about how things are with you."

Is she serious? "I had a huge fight with my best friend. I don't want to talk about me. I want to talk about her. We have to help her."

"If she's looking for a good therapist, I'm sure I can find a good referral. Now back to you."

"Charlotte doesn't need a therapist. She has me. You just have to help me figure out a way to let her know she's making a big mistake."

"And you know what's best for her?"

I cross my arms in front of my chest. Someone should tell ET that sarcastic therapy is passé.

"Maybe that's what you're missing," she says. "A bossy and judgmental friend."

How dare she? "I'm not bossy!"

"Then why do you think you should be telling her what to do?"

"She was finally getting over him. And he's sucking her back to the same drama."

"You said he's divorced now. Doesn't sound like he's sucking her back to the same drama at all. It's up to her to decide if it's what she wants."

"She deserves better."

"Why does it bother you if she thinks giving him a chance is the right thing for her?"

"Once a cheater, always a cheater."

"But he won't be cheating on you. So why are you so mad at her?"

"I'm not mad at her. I'm worried. He really doesn't deserve her."

"How do you know?"

"He's not into her, into her life, what's good for her. He's just taking care of himself."

"Maybe that's why you don't like him."

"Because he's selfish, self-centered...?"

"He's chasing his dream. And so is she. And that's bugging the shit out of you."

These words sound familiar. Charlotte's words, from the other night. I fold my arms tighter across my chest and refuse to speak.

"Perhaps," she says, "you're jealous."

"How could I be? I hate him. And I love Charlotte."

"I know you love her," she says, gently. Finally.

Why is it when she gets gentle, I always have the overwhelming urge to cry? "So I'm a little jealous of her guts. Any logical person knows this isn't a good idea. And Charlotte's very intelligent. Deep down, she knows it, too. But it doesn't matter. She's going for it anyway."

I lean forward in my chair, resting my head in my hands. "I can't even go for my smart ideas. I play it safe, look at everything from every possibility, hedge all my bets. And then I still don't go for it." I look up. "I bought a stupid car. I cut off all my hair. What have I changed? Nothing. I'm just pretending to be someone I'd like to know." I sit back again. "Why can't she be more like me? Buy a new car. Cut her hair. Well, not her hair, she's got these glorious curls, but...get a tattoo. Why does she have to throw her whole life away?"

"She doesn't think she's throwing her life away."

"She's making a mistake. Choices we make in life are like nails in coffins. Sure, a few nails here and there and you can still kick yourself free. But with each nail, it gets a little harder. She's going to go down there. It will be all romantic for a while. He's got kids. She's going to fall in love with them. And they'll love her. Soon, before she knows it, she'll be stuck. Trapped. And she won't be able to get out."

"Julia, do you see you're not talking about Charlotte? Charlotte doesn't feel trapped. She's not asking for help. You're asking why can't she be more like you, but I hear your question another way. Do you want to know the question I think you really want to ask?"

No. Hell, no. When her voice gets quiet like this, I know I am in trouble.

"Why can't you be more like her?"

Having someone else ask the question that has been playing hide-n-seek in my subconscious pierces my denial and resistance. Awareness explodes in me like a gunshot. "You want to know why I can't be like her?" I practically scream. "Why I can't be like you, going to a yoga retreat in Hawaii? Why I can't shed identities like Eva? You want to know the difference between me and all the women in my life that are giving me the same advice?" I don't wait for her to answer. "You don't have families! You can fall apart when you don't have a family. You can fall apart and take your sweet time putting yourself back together, even better than before. And that's great. Falling apart is a luxury that all three of you have... because you don't have families!"

I stand up and pace around the small sofa. "Why shouldn't Charlotte go be with Ken? What's the worst that's going to happen? He cheats on her? Sure, she may be heartbroken, but she can start over again. No one else will bear the burden of her choice. Tinkerbell can run off to Never, Neverland and do yoga. What's the worst that can happen to you? You learn how to be a moving cobra, run out of money, and come back and start doing therapy again. At a hundred and forty dollars an hour, it won't take you long to move your downward dog out of the poorhouse."

I drop back into my chair. The sudden burst of energy from my revelation leaves me deflated. Nothing is solved. Now I just know why I am stuck. Still solid, in-the-ground, stuck. "You all can fall down, then pick yourselves up, dust off, and start all over again." I sigh. "I can't do that."

"Why not?" Madelyn asks.

"Because I'm not the only one who falls down. I'm not the only one who faces the consequences of my decisions. Katie. And Michael. They pay, too. So if I make a mistake, it doesn't hurt just me. It hurts the people I love the most. That is the albatross of love."

"So what is the worst that can happen to you, and because of you, to them?"

"First off, I have to take a lot of options off the table. I'm not going to move and take Katie out of high school and make her start over. So moving is off the table for the next however many years. And I can't go for broke and not worry about money, can't spend it all, can't spend savings, can't even spend everything I make because of the exorbitant price of college. I need to be saving. So moving is off the table. And making a huge mistake in love not an option. If I marry Michael, his income counts against Katie getting money for college. If I leave Michael, I'm teaching her to abandon people. She'll either have abandonment issues or commitment issues. Either way, it will be all my fault."

"So you and Michael have nothing to do with, well, you and Michael. Your financial life is basically a calculation for Katie's college fund. And your love life is nothing more than the setup of Katie's future emotional issues."

I sigh, ignoring her sarcasm. She doesn't understand. How can she? She doesn't have a family. "I'd better stay right where I am," I say softly. "At least I can say that I'm doing the least amount of damage to my family."

"So Katie and Michael are the nails in your coffin?"

"It sounds terrible, I know..."

"Aren't they convenient for you?"

"Convenient? Haven't you been listening?"

She looks at me long and hard to make sure I am listening. "You're using the family you say you love as your noble, ready-made excuse to settle for less than the life that you want."

Her little bell goes off. My time is up.

Chapter Fifteen

I knock on my condo door. Maybe Maggie is wrong. Maybe my tenant, who hasn't paid her rent for the last three months, is waiting for me, the rent neatly stacked in large bills on her pretty marble table.

Not.

No one answers. My knock has a rather hollow sound, so I casually bump the door knob. It's unlocked, just like Maggie said. And the rooms are completely empty.

I just can't do this anymore.

I've been through this twice before. My first tenant stayed a couple of years. I kept their rent low. I told them, and my subsequent tenants, that I would never raise their rent. My mortgage wasn't going to go up, and it was worth keeping a good tenant.

Having someone cover the mortgage is my savings plan for Katie's college.

I want to throw myself on the floor and have a good old tantrum but the carpets are too dirty. I am not surprised they need to be replaced. They are the same carpets that had been there when I bought the place ten years ago. The walls need to be painted. Sinks and cabinets and counters cleaned. Window frames scrubbed.

I have never been a quitter. I've always been proud of the fact that I am the type that can, and will, do whatever needs to be done. As I stand here looking at the empty condo, it surprises me that although unfamiliar, I recognize what I am feeling.

Defeat. Beaten. That whatever you want to call it, I know I have reached the end of this particular rope.

It's one thing to swim too far out into the ocean. Maybe you don't notice the tide is going out, the weather is calm, and you're a good swimmer. It is quite another thing to see waves big enough to knock over a house, know your life vest is in the bottom of the boat, and decide to jump into the water anyway because you are hot. In other words, it's one thing to drown by accident. It's something entirely different to knowingly drown.

I pull my cell phone out of my purse, find the name of the realtor who had helped us with our house, and dial her number.

"I've got an empty condo and I just don't know what to do with it anymore," I say when she answers.

"Give me the address," Angela says, all business. "I'll be there in twenty minutes. Can you wait?"

Wait for rescue? Do I have a choice? I don't know how I did it before, I don't know why this time is different, and I don't know why I can't find the strength. I don't care that I might have help at the studio. I don't care that I should be able to do it. The only thing I do know is I can't.

"I'll wait."

Half an hour later, I follow Angela around the condo. "This is my savings plan," I explain. "Katie's college fund. My plan is to keep it until she goes to college..."

"But you're tired of being a landlord," she says, walking around, her eagle eyes not missing anything. The broken light. The missing cabinet handles.

"I hardly think of myself as a landlord with only one rental," I said, trailing along behind her.

"It's like having kids. Once you get one, it's official. Mother, landlord, once you have one, you might as well have another." She writes things down in her notebook, checklists that I can see standing at attention like little soldiers, eager to get their turn to be crossed off. They wouldn't dare defy their commanding officer. I have the urge to salute her.

"We can fix it up and rent it out again, if that's what you want. My company has a rental division. They charge one month's rent to do the whole application process, including a background check on prospective tenants. Either way, you need to get this place cleaned up. New carpets. You could probably get away with not painting the second bedroom, but since everything else has to be done..."

She might be making the list, but I am the one who has to do it all. Clean it up. Fix it up. "My daughter's going to be away next week and I've got a few days off. I can get in here and start to..." The words *I can do it* come out of my mouth by habit... without my permission. Why won't I listen to the part of me that is screaming, "*I can't do it!*"

"Who says you have to do it?" she asks.

I laugh when I really want to cry. "Because there's no one else."

"Are you kidding? We can hire a cleaning company. With a crew of two or three, they can be out of here in a day. Spic and span."

"Really? How much?"

"Say you have two people, for an afternoon. At twenty dollars an hour, I'd say roughly two hundred."

Two hundred dollars? And I didn't have to scrub a toilet someone else has been using? "Do it!"

She adds it to her list. "And I've got a great jack-of-all-trades. He can get in here, paint, fix the light in the bathroom, fix the drawers—"

"Yes!"

She pulls out her cell phone and calls her office. "Call John," she says to her secretary. "See if he's available for a couple days. Tell him to give me a good quote and he can start tomorrow." She hangs up.

"Tomorrow?"

"He'll paint first, so we can get new carpets in here—"

"And then what am I going to do? Am I selling? Am I renting again?" The thought of renting again feels like chronic constipation. But the thought of selling makes me want to throw up.

"Let's start by cleaning it up. You've got time to decide which way to go."

Time. Time to waffle. Time to doubt myself.

"Julia, you've got to take the emotion out of this."

Easy for her to say.

"If this really is just an investment, then we look at it logically."

Logical? Me?

She flips her notebook open to a clean page and draws a line down the middle. "Okay, how old is Katie?"

"Fourteen."

"So she'll be going to college in four years." She writes the amount of rent I have been charging and multiplies it by forty-eight months. "If you rent it, you'll make this," she says, showing me a figure.

"Okay?"

"Now of course, we don't know what the market will do. But you bought this in the eighties, when the market was really low. It's doubled in value since you bought it, and we know that isn't going to happen again in the next ten years. And you told me more than half the mortgage is paid off, so if you sell it now, and put that money in an account, making say, five percent interest..." Her pencil flies across the page. "Seems like you'll break even."

"Break even?"

"That's assuming it's rented all the time between now and then. And you don't have any problem with tenants not paying. And not running off," she adds.

"Break even?" I repeat.

She smiles. In her business, she probably sees the dumb look that is pasted to my face often. "Without the headache of renting," she adds.

Katie would be taken care of. And I'd be off one hook. "Do it."

"You're sure?"

"Of course I'm not sure." I'm not sure about anything. I don't even remember what "sure" feels like. Taking care of Katie's college is the only thing that matters to me. That isn't something I am willing to gamble with. "Sell."

She pulls her phone off her belt clip. She talks to me, waiting for the person on the other end to pick up. "There are three other units in this complex up for sale. I've seen two of them. They're the standard white walls, beige carpets. You've got an end unit, which is good, but they've got more square footage. I think we should make yours different. Make it homey. Relaxing, like a spa."

I nod.

"We'll stage it."

"Like those television shows?"

Angela nods and talks into the phone, my own little bulldozer at work. "And call the furniture rental place, and see how much it would cost to rent, let's see, a sofa, not too big, a mahogany entertainment center, a round kitchen table and chairs, and one queen bed."

I touch her elbow. "We have an extra bed I could bring over."

"Cancel the bed," she says and hangs up, writing feverishly.

A bird in the hand... I will take the money, put it in a safe account for Katie's education, permanently retire as a landlord...

And rest easy.

My cell phone rings and I think about leaving it in my purse. I can't think of anyone I want to talk to. Charlotte sure as hell won't be calling, not that I want to talk to her anyway. I don't care if I ever speak to her again.

But what if Katie needs me? I mean, really needs me. Not just for a ride, but what if she's hurt? What if something is seriously wrong?

"Hello," I say, not even looking at the caller ID. Who knows what number will show up from the hospital anyway?

"Are you almost here?"

Eva! "You're not going to believe what my tenant ..."

"Tell me when you get here," she interrupts.

"Where?" Were we supposed to meet for lunch and I forgot?

"The lesson. With Phillip. And Marco."

"Oh, shit. I totally forgot, Eva. There's been a lot going on—"

"As I said: tell me when you get here."

"I'm really not in the mood to dance," I say, knowing I am whining—hoping it will get me off the hook.

"What are you doing instead?" she asks.

Let's see. I'm thinking about driving home, pulling into the garage and doing my own middle-aged version of that Whitesnake video from the eighties where the hot girl with the long red hair dances seductively on the hood of the lead singer's car. In my video, the star—that would be me—has short red hair. And instead of dancing seductively on a moving car, I'm going to just flop myself back in the seat of a parked car and take a nap.

"You promised Phillip, and I can't get anyone else on such short notice," Eva says, interrupting my version of a good MTV video. "Plus, I think you need it as much as Phillip does."

"I don't have any dance shoes with me. And I've got jeans on." I should have tried this excuse first. Eva was much more apt to buy an I-don't-have-the-right-thing-to-wear excuse.

"You can wear my shoes."

Damn.

"And you can borrow something of mine."

Tempting. "I get to go in your closet? Carte blanche?"

"Yes," she says, knowing she has me hooked. "Just get your tapping toes over here!"

Chapter Sixteen

Along one wall of Eva's office she has a huge wardrobe, the kind in children's fantasy movies where you could open the heavy wooden doors, step through, and be transported to another world. The inside of her closet is stuffed with costumes—ball gowns in a rainbow of colors, decorated with hundreds of sparkling rhinestones and trimmed with feathers. And sexy Latin costumes with cutouts and fringe. When I was a child I felt perfectly comfortable raiding Eva's closet because I believed I was a princess.

As I open the doors now, the double mirrors gang up on me, laughing at me, taunting me... *Imposter! Poser!* Phillip is right. I'm a soccer mom. Looking in the mirror, I don't even do soccer moms justice.

Eva comes into her office and closes the door behind her. "You better hurry up. Phillip is working himself into a tizzy."

"Eva, I don't know what I'm doing here."

"You're doing tango," she says.

I didn't mean I don't know what dance I am supposed to do, and she knows it.

"So you need simple. Elegant. Strong."

Simple? I might be able to pull that off. Elegant? Strong? Unless she has a suit of armor bejeweled with rhinestones...

She pulls a couple of black things out of her closet and throws them at me. "You have sixty seconds before I'm back." she says, closing the door behind her, the threat clear that she will drag me out of her office, whatever I have on.

Knowing she means it, I rip off my jeans, yank my T-shirt over my head, and dive into the outfit. Whatever it is, it's better than what I'm wearing.

True to her word, she returns while I am still zipping the skirt. "Honey-child, you can't wear a bra with this bodysuit." She whips me around and I see my white Bali bra strap slicing across my back.

I slip the faded bra off and pull the sleeves of the bodysuit back onto my shoulders. Eva stands back and studies me, her thumb under chin in the classic thinker pose. She reaches into her overflowing wardrobe and grabs a scarf with embroidered red roses and long black fringe. She ties it around my hips and uses her fingers to slick my short hair behind my ears. She smiles at me, stands on her tiptoes and kisses my forehead, then turns me around.

In the mirror, I see a glimpse of the woman I want to be, the one I imagine I could be, the one I want to find. I am wearing a long, black, silk chiffon skirt that swirls around my legs and a black bodysuit with soft butterfly sleeves. When I turn, a very low, scooped back completes the look of a woman who feels confident and sure. If only I had known this woman was hiding in Eva's closet.

On the inside, I know I'm still a mess, still a woman who's lost her best friend, still a woman who wants to end it all with a nap.

But on the outside... "I am going to beg, borrow, or steal this outfit from you," I say. "If I wear it long enough, maybe I'll believe my own picture." Hell, at the very least, I want to be buried in it.

"Consider it yours," she says, my very own fairy godmother. "Now get moving." She hands me a nude colored pair of dance shoes. "Phillip is in the back ballroom. He's got the music on but he's moving around like he can't remember his own routine."

I slip the shoes on my feet. Although they have a heel, of course, I am thankful they aren't too high. I go into the studio and Phillip does a double take, clutching his chest for effect. "Wow! You do tip the scales at attractive," he says, raising one eyebrow, "if you go for the femme fatale type."

Me? Femme fatale? I must look better than I think. I almost giggle but I doubt femme fatales giggle so I purr instead, an Eartha Kitt growl in the back of my throat. I forgot I knew how to do that.

"I can't remember the first eight counts of the opening," he says.

"It's hard to do it by yourself," I say, getting into dance position with him. I start moving and his muscle memory kicks in. It feels strange being in a dance studio to dance, to really dance myself... like a foreign language that I am supposed to know from another life.

We are in the middle of a lunge when Phillip freezes. Has he forgotten the next part?

Phillip straightens his leg and we are both upright. I turn around, and suddenly know why Phillip stopped.

Imagine James Bond and Rambo have somehow mated and produced the perfect man.

Marco.

He walks gracefully, smoothly, like a cat. With his dark hair and blazing blue eyes, he could be a vampire promising an intense bite filled with a potent blast of pleasure. And sweet, delicious pain. I have the urge to throw my neck back and whisper, "Bite me."

The most powerful, understated presence I have ever seen in a man.

He has long hair, well, long for a ballroom dancer. Soft black waves that dance along the collar of his shirt. I can feel Phillips fingers just itching to touch it. Hell, I'm not a hairdresser and I want to run my fingers through Marco's hair.

Black, fitted trousers encase his legs and hips. And his butt! He has a butt tight enough to rest a cup of tea on. In England, they had determined that doing a round of the five standard dances was like running a sub-four-minutes mile. Of all the athletes in the world, give me a dancer's body any day. Flexibility combined with strength and endurance. Dancers have it all. This man has it all. And then some.

"Hi. My name is Marco," he says, reaching out his hand as he introduces himself. Oh God. An Italian accent.

Phillip lets go of me like I have the plague, stepping in front of me to shake hands with Marco, as if touching him first means he can claim him. Then Marco turns to me. "And I hear you're Eva's niece," he says, leaning forward to kiss both my cheeks with European flair.

"Yes. Julia. Julia Stone."

He looks at me, studying me for a second. "Have we met before?" he asks. "Maybe another time I was here?"

I try to pretend it's possible. Try to pretend that I could have met him... and forgotten him. It would be like the Pope pretending he didn't know God when he got to the pearly gates. "No. We've never met."

He shrugs his shoulders. My God, even his shrugs are graceful.

"Eva says you are working on a routine," he says. He walks over to the stereo. "I'll start your music over."

Right to business. That's good. Business. Routine. Dance. Oh, my!

While Marco gets our music ready, I whisper to Phillip, "Whose team does he play for?"

"I don't know. And stop that. If I start thinking that way, I'm not going to be able to dance. That's why you're here. To keep things desexed."

I sniff, pretending to be miffed. I'm not so sure I like the idea of being a sex neutralizer. I've just come out of the closet, Eva's proverbial closet, and I'm certainly not ready to go back in.

The music starts and we go through the whole routine. We don't make any big mistakes, but it certainly isn't the best we've danced.

"I should probably tell you," Phillip says when we finish, "Julia just learned this last weekend. My regular partner is away. I wanted a lesson with you, so Julia was nice enough to fill in."

Why is he making excuses for me?

"You both did fine," Marco said.

Fine? Fine in dance-speak means you phoned it in.

They are both right. I went through the motions correctly, but I hadn't danced. I could feel my own ghost haunting me, reminding me of a time when I used my body as an instrument to express the music, not just tread water. I am trying so hard to do everything right, that I forget the most important part. I forget to dance.

"Let me, let us do it again," I say. "I know we can do it much better."

"The good news is...it's never about your partner." Marco shuts the music off and comes over to us. "Even if you have the same partner for your whole dance career, they're always different. Different moods, different energy levels, different ideas on dance. You can't control anything about your partner."

"Amen to that," Phillip says. "In dance. Or in love." He chuckles. "So I can't blame her in the middle where I'm always off balance? I'm either too forward, or when I fix that, I'm back-weighted."

"Phillip, do you know what your center is?"

"My center...?" Phillip repeats the words slowly.

Marco laughs. I didn't know you could laugh with an accent. "I'm not trying to trick you," he says.

I had found my center, a long time ago. As surely as I found it, I seem to have lost it again. Maybe there's a lost and found for dancers?

"It's your core muscles," Phillip blurts out.

"That's a great answer," Marco says. "Your center is a term dancers throw around a lot, and I never really knew what they meant. So one day, I asked my coach. He said, "You cut yourself in half this way,"" Marco makes a horizontal slash across the middle of Phillip's body, "and in half this way," a vertical slash this time, "and the place those two cuts meet is your center." Marco smiles. "Now I was willing to do just about anything to become a great dancer, but I was pretty sure cutting myself in half was going to be more of a hindrance than a help. A couple years later, I heard the best definition."

Phillip is all ears now.

Marco pulls me over, turning my body so I am sandwiched between the two men. "Can I use your body?" he asks me.

Gulp! Use my body? But one look at Marco's face and I know he is serious. I nod, not trusting words.

"You have four body blocks of weight," he explains. "Hips." He touches my hips so gently I feel like his fingers are whispering to my pelvis, a snake charmer waking up the sleeping serpent coiled at the base of my spine.

"Ribs," he continues. His fingers move up, the tips of his fingers like a match lighting a path from my hips to my ribs, opening me. My heart beats a primal rhythm as it is set free in my expanded ribcage.

"Shoulders," he says. His strong hands move to my shoulders, lifting me straighter, taller than I have ever stood before.

"And head," he finishes, his hands on either side of my head like in the old movies, just before they kiss.

I swallow and try to control my breathing. I feel like I have just surfaced and can't get enough air.

"You stack these four body blocks, like threading four Lifesavers onto a toothpick, lining up the holes of the Lifesavers. It's only when you line your body blocks up that your body can really communicate with itself. The intangible—your spirit— is housed by the tangible—your body. That space is your center. The whole purpose of the body is to create this hollow space so that your spirit can dance."

Phillip reaches for me, wanting to try it.

Marco steps between us. "You can't rush. Before you can partner with someone, you have to find your own center." He takes a slow, deep breath and Phillip and I breathe with him. "We all go to partnerships, thinking it's our partner that's going to help us dance the way we want to. Our partner, or our partnership, is going to be our vehicle to great dancing." He takes another breath and turns to me, slowly moving his body from one foot to another, a slow hypnotic movement that I copy without thought. "You," he says, his words caressing to my soul, "have all the power."

"Then why dance with someone else?" I ask, knowing this man could be fatal to the old me. The new me. The parts I don't like... and the parts I do.

"Because if you bring all of you, and I bring all of me, then that's when the magic can happen. Together we can do more than we could ever do alone."

I feel him find his own center, and I look for mine.

"And I'm not just talking technique," he says. "No one can know all the technique. But you've got to bring everything you have." He reaches his left hand towards me, inviting me into his arms.

I move into dance position. What if I can't follow? What if I don't know what he's trying to do? He stops me, holding me away from him so gently that I think I might cry in frustration. His hands are still on me, not to keep me away, just reminding me to find my center first. "You have to take the time to be in your own body," he says looking at me, "before you can be with anyone."

I swear, if I become any more aware of my body I will self-combust.

"Aware of your own balance," he says softly, seducing me into my own body.

He releases his hold on me, opening his arms again. "Once you find yourself, if you feel like it, dance with me."

I close my eyes and take a deep breath, feeling the air move inside my body, looking for that hollow that holds my spirit.

Then he touches me. And I know him.

I can actually feel his loneliness. I open my eyes and see us in the mirror, two halves to a whole. Both dressed in black, I can't tell where he finishes and I begin yet I can feel his spirit as clearly as I see his perfect blue eyes.

Marco's inner turmoil doesn't penetrate his years of practiced control. His quiet acceptance feels like defeat and I want to cry for him. My struggle has been leaking out of my body and spilling all over my life. While it may not be as pretty and dignified, I choose to fight the ache rather than accept it. Suddenly, my ranting and raving feels brave and I yearn to resist even more.

Phillip must have turned the music on because suddenly the aggressive beat of the tango fills my body until my heart is beating a slow, slow, quick, quick, slow rhythm. I'm not dancing tango. I am being danced. The steps with Phillip have rung a familiar but distant bell. Dancing with Marco is like a portal to heaven.

"You're like an explosion of emotion," he says, sounding even more surprised than me. The music is building and he ups the challenge, doing more difficult moves. He moves, and I move faster. He wants tighter turns, and I make them tighter yet. When he spins me out of his arms, still holding one hand, I wrap myself back into his arms like a dancing tornado, our bodies pivoting to the music together.

Beat one. Step forward.

Two. Step back.

Three. Forward.

Four. Back.

The music is building to a crescendo with cymbals. Five. Six. Seven. I throw myself into a dip on the final, crashing note of the music.

He holds me in the dip, not letting me up, even after the music stops. "How did you know I would catch you?" he asks softly in my ear.

"You couldn't not catch me."

Chapter Seventeen

"Mom! Did you buy me sunscreen?"

Of course I did. "I put it right on top of your dresser."

"Did you get the spray kind I like?"

No. I got the kind you hate. "Of course I did."

"Mom!"

Fingernails on a chalkboard.

"Where is the suitcase?" Katie yells from upstairs. "The one with the wheels?"

I take a breath and count to five. "In the closet in the extra bedroom."

"Mom! Can I take your phone charger since mine is broken?"

"Of course you can." I'll just use Michael's charger. Of course, he uses it overnight so I'll have to remember to charge mine during the day, i.e. my phone won't be charged. Since I won't be talking on my phone much, maybe I can get to the hardware store to buy some of that plastic coating that is supposed to be around the wires in my brain so I don't get mini-electrocuted every time I hear...

"MOM!" Katie runs into the kitchen to grab a snack. "Is it okay if I take all the apples?"

I hold my breath and nod.

She can't wait to go. She is vibrating with excitement.

I can't wait for her to go. I am racked with guilt.

She runs back up to her room to finish packing, and I sigh. I swear I know what a wolf in a trap feels like when it realizes the only hope of escape is to gnaw off its own leg. If she wasn't leaving for Florida today, I would have to ask her to call me Julia because if I hear Mom one more time, I think the blood vessels in my eyes will pop.

I also know ten years from now I'll give anything to have my fourteen-year-old Katie in the kitchen asking me to give her a ride.

So why can't I enjoy the moment now?

Because I feel guilty that Katie's going on vacation with another family, without me. I lean back on the counter. True, I do feel guilty. I am the judge and jury and the gavel is pounding inside my head, giving me a headache. Guilty of not being the kind of mom that wants to go to Disney World. Guilty that as a working mother, I don't spend enough time with Katie.

But mostly guilty of feeling relief.

So relief and grief, the rhyming duo, are today's civil war inside me.

I try to rationalize the guilt away with the idea that I am going to use this week to clear my plate. I've got the two interviews set up at the studio tomorrow and Angela called yesterday. My condo is cleaned and painted, and the rental furniture has been delivered. I just need to bring over the curtains so Angela can take pictures and get that condo on the market.

Landlord title... gone.

Lots of responsibilities at the studio... going, going, gone.

I'm going to clear my head, clear my plate, and clear my heart so the important things in life have room to grow.

By the time Katie comes back, I'll be dying to hear... "Mom!"

Marco's voice reverberates in my head.

How did you know I would catch you?
You couldn't not.

Now is not the time to be thinking about dancing. With Marco.

But it's been so long since someone caught me. I've been catching everybody. Catching Katie before she falls. And if I don't catch her, I'll be there to make it all better with a kiss.

I can't help but wonder if Marco had dropped me, would he have kissed me all better?

"Mom..."

I jump, spilling lukewarm decaf coffee on my blouse.

"We really should get going. I thought you were going to put my backpack in the car."

I grab her backpack, a wet paper towel to dab my blouse, and my purse.

As we drive to the airport, I listen to her excited chatter. Her enthusiasm is like smoke, trying to cling to me. I fight it off. Flat Julia is on my dash, smiling. She is listening to Katie go on and on about the trip...about how excited she is to fly, hoping she'll get a window seat, hoping the slide at the water park is as big as it looks online. Flat Julia smiles through it all.

Smiling at Katie... smirking at me. "Why don't you learn a thing or two from your daughter here?" Flat Julia says in my head. "Life isn't all bad. It isn't out to get you. There're lots of great things in life, if you just look for them. In your case, the good things are biting you in the ass, and you're still complaining."

"How do we know she isn't going to grow up to be just like me?"

"Julia," she says with the patience of a saint, "would that be such a bad thing?"

An annoying saint. "Then I should tell her. Enjoy life now, Sweetie. Enjoy it while you can."

"So far," Flat Julia says, "good advice."

If she's not catching my sarcasm, then I can't help but wonder if she's listening to Katie more than she's listening to me.

"Your twenties will be about breaking free. Going out on your own, becoming independent, enjoying your freedom.

long, or that it will be fabulous and you'll stay there forever."

"Twenties are looking good," Flat Julia says.

I'm sure of it. Flat Julia is humoring me. She's my damn image, and even she finds me boring.

I continue anyway, in my head. "In your thirties, you'll probably start a family, confident that you'll do it so much better than your family before you. Confident in ideals such as 'love can conquer all.' That 'life will be fair.'"

I want to wipe the smile off her paper face. "And then your forties come along and you hit the wall of reality like a high speed car hitting a wall of bricks. You'll be like a garden stone statue frozen in fear on the diving board of life. An aura of sadness, of regret, of disappointment, of something will color everything you see—"

"I don't know about this..." Flat Julia says.

I finally have her attention.

"Until you start talking to pictures of yourself because you need a reminder, any reminder, that at one time, you liked yourself!"

Flat Julia is quiet.

"Do you have your camera?" I ask. "You're going to want to take lots of pictures, and make sure you get yourself in some of them." I'm talking to Katie, but I'm scoring points against Flat Julia.

"Mom, my phone is my camera. Haven't you been listening?"

"Of course I have, sweetie." Flat Julia and her Pollyanna version of growing up. Easy for her to think it's going to be all chocolate and roses. Stuck in Photoland, Flat Julia never had to grow up.

We park and hustle along the sidewalk outside American Airlines. Katie is walking with quick little steps to avoid being bumped by her overstuffed suitcase. I trail behind with her backpack slung over my shoulder, my own invisible luggage keeping me grounded. Guilt. What kind of mother can't wait for her only child to leave on vacation?

"Mom!" she cries, looking at the departure board. "I can't find my flight."

"It's got to be up there, sweetie," I say in my calmest mother voice, my eyes darting all over the departure board. Inside, I'm having a worse tantrum than she would even know how to throw. If those flight people have any idea what's good for them, they will keep Katie's flight running smoothly and on time. A mother letting her child go, balancing on the edge of relief and guilt, is more trouble than they can handle. "There it is," I say.

"Katie! Julia!" Emily's family is all gathered at the checkin counter. Father, mother, twin girls, Emily, and assorted luggage. A picture of them all gathered with their smiling faces should be embossed on the center of a dartboard for the rest of us who aren't quite living up to the American dream.

We join the group, and Emily and Katie run off to the gift store to buy postcards of Boston to send to themselves, marking the beginning of their adventure.

Tina smiles, watching the girls like a hawk. "It won't be long until they're off to college." I can hear the wistfulness in her voice. "What will we do when our little nests are empty?"

First of all, I want to remind her that nests are made of vomit and shit. That's the glue that holds a nest together. And we have four years before Emily and Katie are going anywhere farther than Disney World. Since the twins are four years younger, her nest won't be empty until the cows come home. And she's spending this week, twenty-four seven, with them. Right now, she's ODing on kids, and she's worried about not getting her fix in say, eight or nine years?

I nod, pretending I understand what she's talking about. I may be a bad mother for looking forward to a week without a plug in the drain that is my daughter, but this woman is an addict. For the first time, I feel like the healthier mother standing next to her.

The girls come back, the luggage gets checked, and suddenly it's time. Time for me to let her go.

My DNA takes over and I don't want her to go. I don't care if she's going to have fun; I don't care if it will give me a chance to get organized. I hug her longer than she wants. The best thing in my life is leaving.

I brush her bangs out of her face. "Did you pack the sunscreen I got you?" I ask, saying anything I can think of to postpone her going.

"Don't worry," Tina says. "We've got plenty."

You've got plenty of *your* sunscreen, I want to say. She needs *my* sunscreen. I'm her mother. I provide the protective coating to keep her from being burned by the world.

Katie nods, and for one tiny second, I see the doubt in her eyes, too. Her hands are still on my arms. I want to cry, recognizing the civil war that is just starting in her little body. Wanting to go. Not wanting to go.

So I step up to the plate. "Sweetie, you're going to have a great time. And call me every night."

Her fingers slip a little. There's nothing like a mother's protective love that makes a kid want to break free. It takes every bit of will that I have not to catch her.

"And make sure you're polite."

She lets go a little more.

"And know that I love you with all my heart," I whisper.

She throws her arms around my neck for a final hug. "I love you, too, Mom."

M.o.m. Three letters. One word.

My whole heart.

Chapter Eighteen

My very first interview and I have found my Girl Friday. I shake hands with Lily as she leaves my office. She is perfect! She's home from college for the summer. And she's majoring in computers, with a minor in small business. She is excited about setting up a computer system, updating all the records. She even promises to get three estimates for me to choose from for refinishing the wood floor.

I wish I could cancel my second appointment, but Natalie is due in ten minutes. I copy another one of the employment applications I picked up at the office supply store onto Julia Stone's Tap Academy stationery. I had worn my only suit jacket. I tried to wear the matching skirt but the damn thing was too tight and felt old fashioned anyway. The jacket still fit, so I paired it with white linen pants. Businesslike, yet still casual.

One thing I learned at Eva's studio yesterday is that looking the part is one step, maybe a cheating step but a step nonetheless, toward actually *being* the part.

Natalie knocks gently on my open office door. Damn. My screening process sucks. When I got her message, I didn't even bother to think which mother was Toby's mom. I figured she was one of the moms who just wanted to make a little extra money over the summer. If I had paid attention, I never would have brought her in for an interview.

Toby's mom is a lawyer, the one who was always on the phone in the waiting room looking at the siblings as if she was one step away from yelling, "Can't you see I'm on the phone!"

I shake her hand and gesture to the seat Lily has just vacated. Natalie's suit certainly isn't old fashioned. The crisp cranberry material is striking with a gold toned camisole and the gold earrings.

I hand her the application and a pen, a formality really. There is no way I am hiring someone who looks like she should be my boss.

She starts filling out the application, quickly and efficiently, barely looking at it. Clearly, a multitasker. "Julia, I'm going to be honest. I am not here for the summer position."

No shit, Sherlock. I don't know what you are here for, but it certainly isn't to work for me for a couple of weeks. Your leather satchel probably cost more than I'm paying for the whole summer.

"I feel like I've known you a long time. Toby started taking classes when she was three. So I've been coming here every week for seven years. And I've always been impressed with everything you do here," she says, her hands folded neatly in her lap. "And I've watched you, too."

I raise an eyebrow.

"It was either watch you or get depressed looking at all those perfect mothers."

"Perfect mothers?"

"Have you ever sat in your waiting room?"

"Can't say that I have."

"The mothers are all out there," she continues, "either knitting or taking care of another child. Some are even nursing. And they've all got this Madonna-like smile, and I don't mean the pop singer, I mean the perfect mother Madonna. They all look so happy. In their jeans, not to be confused with dungarees, and their pastel pretty tops."

I have to admit, I never thought of my waiting room as a competitive sport, but I certainly know the feeling of looking at another mother and finding myself lacking.

"Anyway," she says.

I add *focused* to the list of adjectives I'm creating for her in my head.

"I've seen you grow this studio in a very competitive market. There are five other dance studios in this town alone."

Sheesh. Last I checked, okay it was probably four years ago, but there was only one other studio. I better get on the ball.

"You hire good teachers, offer a wide variety of classes, and have a huge recital at the end of the year. Just when the little girls are getting tired of going to dance every week, you give them," she smiles and clears her throat, "well, you charge the parents a rather exorbitant rate for a pretty little costume, then get the girls signed up quick for next year. Brilliant marketing, I must say."

I feel complimented, and pressured, all at the same time.

She hands me the application, and I pretend to look it over.

"So last week, when I saw your ad on the bulletin board, I knew exactly what is happening here. You are starting to feel the same. Like you can't measure up."

<u>Starting</u> to feel that way?

"I know the feeling. I feel like I'm not measuring up in either world, the work world or the mommy world. I graduated valedictorian from high school. Summa cum laude from college. Passed the bar my first time. I'm an exceller. But ever since I had Toby, I'm a compromiser."

Amen to that. I am finding the juxtaposition that is Natalie more fascinating than I'd like to admit. Here I am thinking if I looked the part, that I would be one step closer. But Natalie couldn't look more professional, yet she is baring her soul, and although it may have a Louis Vitton label, she is a bit of a mess. Sharp dresser. Focused. And a mess. I'm starting to like her. A little.

But I'm not stupid enough to think having her in my studio is a good idea. It would be like having a Victoria Secret model in your closet at home in the morning to help you pick out your clothes. "Good morning, Ms. Stone," the tanned, perky size two

143

would say. "Do you want your old lady jeans today, or let's see..." She'd look around my messy closet, her long blonde hair blowing in the wind that follows her around. "Guess that's the only choice, since nothing else fits you."

Clearly, Lily is much more suited to this job, and to my self-esteem, than Natalie.

I'm about to tell her exactly that, when she says, "So I quit my job. And I'd like to invest in the studio with you."

"What?!" Sharp dresser, focused, bit of a mess, and as crazy and impulsive as... *Charlotte*. My heart contracts a little.

Natalie pulls a packet out of her leather satchel and places it on my desk, right on top of her application. "I don't want to take on the summer project. I want to be your partner."

"Partner?"

"I put together a proposal," she says. "I used the standard business formula for determining what a service business is worth. I invest half that amount, and bingo, we're partners."

Who does she think she is? I am offering a summer, part-time position, and here she is, trying to buy half my business?

"Partnerships work best when responsibilities are clearly divided. You do the dancing. I do the business."

I open the packet.

According to this formula my studio is worth two hundred thousand dollars. I am way more successful than I realized. But what the hell good is it if it's killing me?

Natalie is offering to pay me one hundred thousand dollars, *and* she is going to work at the studio?

"I would draw a salary as business manager, as you would for being Dance Director. And at the end of the year, we split the profits."

I am stunned. "I wasn't looking for a partner. This is the first time I've looked for any help—"

"And for women like us, recognizing we can't do it all is like the first step of a twelve step program."

I smile, still holding the papers. "This is something I am going to need to think about."

"How about you give me the summer job and we look at it as a trial run. See what I can do?"

Although Lily is definitely the straightforward answer to the summer job, Natalie might be a long term solution. And she's not asking for a commitment...

"Deal," I say, reaching out and shaking her hand. "I need you ASAP. Can you start tomorrow?"

She smiles, a Vera Wang smile, elegant and satisfied, and shakes my hand.

Sharp dresser, focused, bit of a mess and ... *my partner*?

Chapter Nineteen

I open the door to my condo hesitantly, peeking through squinted eyes, afraid of what I will see. Angela said the only thing left is for me to bring the bed over. But it had only been a couple of days... how can everything possibly be done?

"Holy moly!" If my key hadn't unlocked the front door, I would swear I am in someone else's condo.

Because this certainly isn't the condo Katie and I lived in for seven years. The living room walls are painted a soft moss green. A cushiony ivory couch sits against one wall and two decorative sconces light the rich mahogany entertainment center from either side. I feel like I have just walked into a relaxing spa and I never want to leave. I slip my sneakers off and grab my cell phone. As soon as Angela answers, I say, "I'd like to make an offer on 507 Heritage Village."

She laughs. "Your condo looks great, don't you think?"

"Hell, yes. It wasn't this pretty when I lived here."

"And you can bet it won't look like that when someone else moves in, either. But that's not our problem. The goal here is to make someone want to live in it."

"You succeeded because I want to live here."

"Did you bring the bed?"

"Michael is bringing it by in a bit in his truck."

"And did you bring linens to match the pale blue walls in the master bedroom?"

I have, but I am not going to put our dark blue comforter in there, even if it is the best one we have. Our best certainly isn't good enough for this beautiful haven. "I'm running to Bed, Bath and Beyond before Michael gets here."

"If you're buying something new, make sure it's something that you want to keep once we sell the condo."

I walk around the condo. "Should I get curtains?" I ask.

"You can if you want to, but I don't think it's necessary." I could hear her smiling into the phone. "It's fun decorating, isn't it?"

Fun had never been a word I would have used regarding decorating. Daunting... disappointing... too much trouble. "And this coffee table?" I say. "It's a work of art." It was a glass table and the legs were wooden carvings of intertwined figures that looked like an abstract tribe of people dancing.

"I found those figures on clearance for ten dollars each. Then I bought the glass and just laid it on top. Be careful, it isn't attached. The rental place sent over a heavy wooden table, but it took up too much room so I sent it back."

"It's beautiful. And those sconces? Where did you get them?"

"In your storage closet."

They do look vaguely familiar. When I bought the sconces years ago, I imagined the living room would look just like this. But when I tried to pick soft green paint, I was terrified I'd end up with mint chocolate chip ice cream smeared on my walls, so I put the sconces away and forgot about my redecorating ideas. Funny how Angela created the room I meant to.

"Don't forget to empty out the rest of the storage closet."

"Thanks for reminding me," I say. "You've done an amazing job here."

She laughs. "I'll come by tomorrow, take pictures, and you should be listed online by tomorrow night."

I thank her again, hang up, and lie down right in the middle of the living room. Angela must have insisted on a good pad. I could probably make snow angels in the lush carpet. Now I want to recarpet our whole house. Except we don't really have much carpet in the house. Mostly hardwood floors. Michael likes hardwood floors, and he sold me by telling me they were easier to clean.

When this condo sells, I am buying another set of sconces, writing down the exact paint color, and stealing this coffee table.

The condo is more than clean. It's had a complete makeover. Our home is once again ready for a fresh start.

I sit up, suddenly aware that I am facing the Time Out Corner. I can see the ghost of two-year-old Katie clearly in my mind, her little bottom twitching, anxious for her time-out to be over.

We had tried the time-out chair but she always got distracted, forgot she was supposed to stay there, and got off the chair. Standing, facing the corner, we took away visual stimulation so she could think about why she was in trouble. But I swear she spent her time practicing her puppy eyes, so I could never stay mad at her.

What I wouldn't give for an adult time-out... a moment to stare into nothing, to think about what I had done, and what I was going to do.

I vaguely remembered the rule I had read in some parenting book. The time out should equal one minute for each year of the child's age. A two-year-old would get a two minute time out, a three-year-old, three minutes. Obviously, a thirty-eight-year-old woman needs a six month time-out. Six months of stillness, six months to think about what she has done wrong, and right, and how she is going to move forward.

A shiver of lightning burns through my veins. My muse. My creativity. A siren song from my spirit, so long forgotten I am surprised she can find me at all.

Time-Out Designs.

I run out to my car and grab the box of dissembled doll limbs that I had taken from Charlotte's house. Then I run down the hall of the building to my storage closet. I scramble to the back and find the box marked "Katie's baby clothes." I saved many of her cutest outfits, hoping someday she would have a daughter and I'd see those precious clothes again. I race back into my condo, find the most assembled doll, and slip a pink dress with tiny French-knotted polka dots over her head. I pull on the matching panties with rows of ruffled lace across the bottom. I stand her up in the corner, resting her head on her arms as she leans against the wall.

Time-Out Dolls.

The niche Charlotte and I have been looking for.

I sit back on my heels and cry.

I cry because I miss Charlotte. I cry because I can't call her, won't call, don't know how to call her.

I cry for Charlotte, wanting nothing more than to call her and tell her that I finally get it. I get why she had to go.

I cry for Katie growing up and starting the process of tearing herself from my heart.

And I cry for me... cry for the constant letting go that is inherent in being a woman. Letting go—when holding on to the people we love is what women are designed to do. When our hearts, and our arms, and our every cell scream that we should hold on... but love requires that we let go.

I wonder... if I stop resisting letting go, will I stop hurting?

And wondering that makes me cry some more.

And when I can't think of anything specific to cry about, I cry for another five minutes.

And feel good about it.

One last big, ragged sigh and I am done. Complete. My tear tank is empty.

I get up and rinse my face in the bathroom. I have half an hour before Michael is supposed to meet me here, so I get in the car and go to Bed, Bath and Beyond. One of the display beds looks like you'd find it in Oprah's bedroom. It's a silver silk cloud.

I buy it. Everything. The silver comforter. The matching shams. (Matching shams! I've never had matching shams!) I buy the decorative pillows. Even the bed skirt. Everything... the works. I can't wait to go home and make my perfect bed.

I get back two minutes before Michael buzzes and I let him in. I meet him out in the hall, holding the door open at the top of the stairs. He has a mattress balanced on top of his head and walks a crooked line up the stairs. He struggles, and he swears, and he refuses my help. At the top of the stairs, he bends his knees and pushes the mattress up like a weightlifter. I grab one end and we lift it over the banister.

He is being very specific with his directions, telling me to go left three feet, then right two, forgetting that we were facing opposite directions so his left is my right. He's directing, and I'm laughing so hard, every time going the opposite way from what he means. The more I laugh, the more he directs, still not understanding that his left is my right. I feel sorry for him and adjust. I go left when he says right, because I know that's what he means.

Last week I would have been so annoyed with this whole process that I would have imagined pushing him over the banister and having the mattress land on top of him, and then jumping up and down on it like a little kid trying to kill the bug under the kitchen towel.

Is it really about choice? Can I choose to be amused, rather than annoyed? Choose to sell half my business, so I can be inspired to start another one?

Michael traps me against the wall in the bedroom, telling me to back up just a little further. Fortunately, the mattress is soft and bends just enough for him to get it around the door frame. The mattress tips over, just inside the heavenly blue bedroom.

I fall on the bed. Suddenly, I feel as fresh as the condo. The past, the future, our issues are erased, if only temporarily. This moment, this space between us, is a blank slate, waiting to be filled.

I grin up at him, patting the bed beside me suggestively.

He hooks his thumbs in his belt loop. "You need to pay me, ma'am. "This moving business ain't cheap," he says, for some reason adopting a southern accent. "Aren't your turned on by my display of masculine strength?"

"I am. But I don't have any money," I say in my best Scarlett O'Hara imitation. "What's a girl to do?"

I pull him down and kiss him like I haven't kissed him in a long while. I've never been the type to romanticize sex. Never called it *making love*. Making love sounds too pretty, too euphemistic to me. Fool around. Have sex. The horizontal mambo. That's what I call it. Today, though, I want to make love with Michael the way I danced with Marco. Every movement fueled by emotion.

Our clothes melt off like well-rehearsed choreography. I feel myself come alive under his touch. His hands stroking the back of my neck make me aware of my neck and my breasts ache for their turn to be touched. He is my other half, my polarity. He is north. I am south. Together, we are the whole world.

In this moment, in this blank space, we are love, lost in lovemaking. Michael is a man. And I am a woman. We fit. We need each other to be what we each are. Without me to hold him, his explosion will disappear. Without him to hold onto, I am without gravity. For a quick moment that feels like forever, just before climaxing, hiding amongst the stars, I get a glimpse of the woman I can be.

Afterwards, we are lying naked, as close as two people can be physically, yet I feel distance creeping in like a silent burglar.

"The condo looks great," he says, pulling his arm out from under my neck. *Houston...Upper body separation completed.*

"How come it didn't look this nice when you lived here?" he asks.

I see two choices in front of me. The first choice, the one I have been making for the past few months or years, is to be annoyed. How patronizing. How condescending. How rude.

But that road seems to lead to angry. Frustrated. And bitchy. So I turn around, making the choice not to go any farther down that road. "Apparently, I'm going to have to take interior decorator off my resume," I joke. Not that funny, though. His left leg wiggles out from under mine.

Houston... appendage one has successfully retracted back to home position.

Astronaut Julia. How's the air up there?

"I guess it's nice," he says, talking about the condo.

Air is a little stale.

"Just not my taste. Not lived in. Too perfect."

"That's the whole point," I say. That is the irresistible beauty of it.

"I like Katie's doll in the corner, though."

I laugh. "It's not Katie's. It's mine."

"Huh?"

"I'll explain later." Explain that I have just created my new business venture. And later might be a good time to tell him I'm thinking about selling half the studio. Not that it is his business, literally, but he is of the old school that says a couple should talk to each other about major decisions. But hell, he came home with a forty-seven inch television after we agreed on a forty-two inch.

That intimacy burglar seems to have lodged itself in my throat. "Charlotte said she wouldn't blame you for cheating on me. She said I hold you away." Why did I insist on bringing our life back into this empty space?

His right leg moves away and I can feel my toes, like a line of little ants, want to follow him. "You didn't used to," he says.

I had hoped he would deny it. Maybe if he did, I could go on pretending things were fine.

"Any idea why you are now?" he asks.

So much for pretending. "I don't know."

"Then I've got a better question," he says, leaning up on his elbow and looking down at me. "Are you almost done?"

I can't repeat myself and say I don't know. So I don't say anything.

Of course that annoys him. I think he hears my silence as not caring. Not caring enough to answer. When the truth is, I honestly have nothing to say.

"How would you like it?" he asks. "How would you like it if I held you at arm's length?"

A question like that is guaranteed to make my mind go blank, a huge black hole of nothing. Would another "I don't know" be better than nothing?

He gets up and pulls his jeans on. "I know. You'd probably like it."

I watch him leave. Why does every interaction I have lately with anyone I love seem to end with them leaving me? Of me having to let them go?

And if I am doing so much of it, why aren't I getting better at it?

I am shocked when he buzzes again. I practically fly to the door to push the button to let him in. He is coming back! Maybe the whole point of letting go is believing they will come back. Maybe if I knew, absolutely knew without a doubt that they'd always come back, maybe then letting go wouldn't hurt so much.

Michael comes in with the second mattress. He manages to get this one in by himself and throws it on top of the other one, a thunder cloud crashing down on the first mattress. He looks at me for a long minute and leaves without a word.

Still naked, I get my perfect linens and make up the bed.

Careful not to disturb anything, I crawl under the covers, my tears spotting the six-hundred-thread-count pillowcase.

Looking in, no one would even know I am here.

Chapter Twenty

An hour later, I am still in the same position when my cell phone rings. Michael...? Calling to say he wants me to stay right here, that he'll come and ravish me, all without messing up the bed.

Or maybe Katie calling to say she wants to come home from Florida early because she misses me so much. But wait. Do I really want that? Amendment: Katie calling to say she misses me so much she <u>wants</u> to come home, but alas, there aren't any flights.

Or Charlotte is calling to apologize from the bottom of her heart, begging me to forgive her for everything she said, and she's moving home tomorrow, and can I please, please, pretend that none of it ever happened.

I pull the cell phone under the covers with me.

"What are you doing?" a voice on the other end says.

Shit! Only Phillip has that annoying twang of an accent. And the audacity not to introduce himself. "Who is this?" I demand. Two can play his game. Note to self... start using the damn caller ID to screen calls.

"It's Phillip and you damn well know it."

"Maybe I do. And maybe I don't." Okay, another note to self... you're not in the second grade anymore.

"Listen, skinny ass—"

Skinny ass? Me? I like this game.

"Seeing you and Marco do my tango routine, I realized that without chemistry, it's nothing. That routine needs sexual chemistry—"

Is he saying that Marco and I had chemistry?

"And I just don't have that with this Paula."

"Are you asking me to be your partner?"

"Hell, no. I've got about as much chemistry with you as I do with an inebriated donkey."

Lovely visual. "So what can I do for you?" I ask.

"Well," he says, starting to sound excited. "I saw Marco at the studio and told him I couldn't dance with either of you donkeys."

"I prefer skinny ass, thank you very much."

"Fine. I told him after watching you and him do porn on the dance floor—"

"You said that to him?" My voice squeaked, like I was in seventh grade. Note to self, you've graduated from middle school, too.

Or at least I thought I did, but I couldn't help myself. "What did he say?"

"He asked who my first choice partner would be. So I told him. I told him I want to dance with my boyfriend, Dan. And guess what he said?"

About me! What did he say about me?

"He said that we could come to his studio in New York. That he's having a showcase and would be honored to have us dance for him. Me and Dan!" I hear him take a deep breath over the phone. "So you've got to get your skinny ass in here and show us everything Marco taught you."

"Okay," I agree, pretending to be reluctant. "But only if you promise to stop calling me skinny ass," I say, knowing he won't be able to resist the bait and he'll keep calling me that.

"Meet us at the studio at five."

Will Marco be there? Flat Julia asks.

Thank God no one else can hear her. Of course Flat Julia is still boy crazy, she hasn't grown up. "I'll be there," I say, smiling as I hang up without saying goodbye.

I've never seen two men dance together and I am not sure what to expect. I like to think I am open minded, but I have to admit, I am having trouble picturing two men doing the tango.

Phillip and Dan are both wearing tuxedos. While Dan's is all black, Phillip's is all white. Both look stunning in their bold choice of color, but together, they are opposites that couldn't exist without the other. We wouldn't know black if we didn't know white. I forget it is two men dancing together. Instead, I see two clear contrasts that together are more interesting than on their own.

I am stunned. As the leader, Phillip hasn't really impressed me. His leads are uncertain, his center of balance, tenuous. As a follower, he literally blossoms into a dancer.

Dan is the opposite of Phillip... quiet, reserved, and even standing with his arms around Phillip in dance position, you aren't sure he is gay. He doesn't have the drama that Phillip has, but even dancing with a man, he possesses a masculinity that Phillip doesn't. Taken singularly, Phillip is a bit too much, and Dan not quite enough. But together, they are balanced.

When they finish dancing, I clap. I cheer. I whistle. I can't show enough appreciation for their creativity... their performance. Their bravery.

"Be honest. What did you think?" Dan asks.

"Too much?" This... from Phillip? I didn't know he thought anything could ever be too much.

I feel honored that I am the first one to see them dance together. "Tango is about passion," I say, "but I've never seen a tango cover the spectrum of passion like you two just did. Strength and power, I mean, that's the obvious part and you both have that in there in spades. But softness... and surrender, that was there, too."

"We did all that? In our tango?" Dan asks, surprised.

"You sure did," I say, meaning every word. "It never occurred to me that I could surrender to passion. I thought passion, and life, and love are all things you chase, and catch with your teeth, and hold onto for dear life." I sigh, still shaking my head. "Surrender to passion... that's really beautiful."

"Think New York is ready to see two men dancing?" Phillip asks.

I lift my shoulders, not sure what to say. "If you're trying to make a statement for gay rights...."

"We're not," Dan says strongly. "Art is supposed to make you see things in a new way. A different perspective. Make you think, and rethink what you already know."

"I know I am blown away, guys. I think New York is lucky to have you."

"Does that mean you'll come to see our debut?" Phillip asks. "It's not that long a drive."

"I don't know," I say. "New York..."

"Just surrender to the urge," Dan teases softly.

I don't surrender to urges. I don't surrender to journeys. At the end of the day, I'm all about crossing things off my To Do list.

"So," Phillip asks again. "Will you?"

Surrender to my urges? They're crazy in a magical, demented, inspiring way. I laugh and throw my arms around them both. "I think I might have to!"

I watch them dance a few more times then go out into the lobby. I pull my cell phone out of my purse and call Natalie. "Can you look on the calendar on my desk and tell me the date of the fall kick-off?" I ask as soon as she answers.

"September 9."

"Okay. Phillip and Dan have put a great tango together and I am going to ask them to dance for us."

"Phillip and Dan?" she asks.

"Yes," I say, hearing the doubt in her voice. "I couldn't picture it at first either, but I just saw them do their routine and it's absolutely beautiful."

"Julia," she says, "I'm sure it is. But you're not an avant-garde art studio, showing the most progressive art here. You're a children's dance studio in the suburbs."

I sigh and let out the breath I've been holding. She's right. I know she's right.

I hate that she is right. The dancer in me wants them to dance at my studio. The business woman in me knows it isn't the right type of promotion. "I just got carried away," I say, hanging up.

I lean my forehead against the window between the lobby and the studio where Phillip and Dan are still dancing. This is the problem with adult life. We're always torn, torn between what we want to do... and what we should do. And as adults, we always go with the safe choice. I am sick of being torn. And I am sick of smart choices.

"I hear you're coming to New York with us."

No need to turn around. Only one man has that gorgeous accent.

I keep watching Phillip and Dan rehearse. There is something very sexy about having a man, a practical stranger, whisper in your ear. Okay, so maybe he's not saying sweet nothings, and maybe he isn't talking about a romantic rendezvous in New York. Not that I'd be interested, of course.

But it is fun pretending. In my mind, he is James Bond and I am a secret spy. Maybe a double agent.

"I'd like to support Phillip and Dan," I say, not committing either way. I turn around. "It's wonderful that you're having them dance for you. We're having a little fall kick-off at my studio and

I wanted to have them dance for us, but my partner is pretty darn conservative. (Okay, she isn't my partner, really, but she wants to be and that's close enough. And it's nice to pretend someone else is making the smart choices.)

"Well then, maybe we can help each other out. If you come to New York and dance with me, in my hour of need," he says with a twinkle in his eye, "I'll come back in the fall and dance with you at your studio."

Is he asking me to dance with him? Shit! What did he just say? Something about hour of need, yadda, yadda, yadda. If I dance with him in New York, he'll dance with me at my studio?

Talk about torn between what I want—dance with Marco!—and the smart choice. The smart choice is to stay home and continue getting my life in order. Deal with the Natalie offer, organize the studio. Oh yeah, and finish breaking down this wall I have with Michael.

"It's a benefit for my wife," Marco says.

"You're married?" *To who? Dancing Barbie?*

"Anna died fifteen years ago. Of breast cancer. We were on the circuit for almost a year. She felt the lump but decided to wait until we got back to the States to check it out. By the time we did, it had progressed."

"My gosh, that's terrible," I say, putting my hand on his arm. Not only a dance hero, but a wounded hero...

"I organized this benefit a few years later and it's gotten bigger every year. I always dance but, as you know, my partner broke her ankle last week, so she can't do it. I suppose I don't have to dance..." he says.

Right. Like he could not dance at the benefit for his dead wife. "There must be someone in New York who can dance with you."

"There is. But I'm going to be here the rest of the week, taking over the lessons my partner can't teach. And the benefit is next weekend."

159

It's been so long since I have done something I know I shouldn't. I remember being sixteen, looking just like Flat Julia, sneaking out of the house to go into the city to my very first concert.

I got caught, but it was worth it to see David Lee Roth in Van Halen.

When I was twenty-five, I married Richard spur of the moment when we were in Vegas doing a show. And that one night, just one night without birth control.

The marriage didn't last. But I have Katie forever.

So every time I did something I wasn't supposed to, I got caught.

I got in trouble.

"And every time, it was worth it," Flat Julia says.

She's right. I stopped taking chances. Maybe it's time I start again. "I'll do it."

Chapter Twenty-One

The very next morning, I plop into Madelyn's chair. "I'm thinking about having an affair," I say.

"You are not."

Evil Tinkerbell with her damn sting.

Okay, maybe I said it mostly for shock value, but who is she not to believe me? "Yes, I am." Doesn't she think I'm wild and crazy enough to have an affair? People a lot more dull than me have affairs all the time...

"With Phillip?" she asks.

"God, no. Phillip's gay." *Hasn't she been paying attention?*

"Well, if you're going to have an affair, why not with a gay guy?"

I look at her strangely. That doesn't even make sense. "With Marco. You know... irresistible, gorgeous Marco. He asked me to dance with him at his benefit. We're going to be dancing together for hours,"—*God, there aren't enough hours in the next week to get me ready.* "Working up a sweat,"—*Why oh why haven't I kept in better shape?*

"You don't want to have an affair with him."

"Why not? I just told you I might."

"That's exactly how I know you're not really thinking about it." She leans forward.

I hate when she leans forward. It usually means she's about to tell me something I don't want to hear.

"This is your pattern. When things get uncomfortable, or a bit too hot to handle, you distract yourself."

161

"What are you talking about?"

"Life isn't as coincidental as it seems. Five years ago, you were avoiding a midlife crisis, and that's when you met Michael. At any other time, you probably wouldn't have considered getting involved with a man that much younger than you. Life threw him in your path when you were vulnerable enough to be open to him."

Wow. Life does that?

"He was a detour," she says. "A distraction."

"Michael isn't a detour. I love him."

"I believe you. But eventually, you have to get back on the main road of your life. And that's where you are now, looking for another detour. Marco. Pretending to think about an affair. Marco is just another distraction."

"So if it's my habit, what makes you think I won't do it this time?"

"Because you can't un-know what you know."

"What if I want to un-know what I know?" I whisper.

She leans closer still, her hands resting on my knees. "What is it you think you know that's scaring you so much?"

"What if I know the second half of my life isn't going to be as good as the first?"

"You don't know that. You're afraid of that. Your fear is speaking loudly. And you are listening so intently that you're finding proof everywhere you look."

I can't help it. I start crying.

"You are so convinced that the second half of your life isn't going to be as good as the first... That Michael isn't going to be as good as your first husband, that another baby couldn't be as good as Katie, that another business would pale in contrast to your dance career, that you are proving yourself right."

"So what do I do?"

"Start listening to your heart. Instead of the fear. And dance with Marco. I promise, you won't have an affair. At least not with him."

I wipe my eyes with a tissue. "If not him, then who?" I joke.

"I'm hoping..." Madelyn says, leaning forward again, "with yourself."

∽∾

I walk into my studio, unlock the door to the business that I started over ten years ago—and I don't recognize the place. The peach walls, the color I have grown to almost hate, are gone. The walls are now painted a silvery grey. Strokes of black paint look like abstract dancers splashed across the wall.

Natalie comes out of the office, a big smile on her face. "What do you think?" she asks.

I'm speechless and her smile fades a bit. "You said you didn't care what color I chose."

Colors like pink. Or yellow. Silver? I said I didn't care what color she painted the lobby. I said I didn't care what color she picked. I didn't say she could do whatever she wanted.

Furious Flat Julia appears on my left shoulder... dressed for battle, brandishing a feathered sword in one hand.

Impressed Flat Julia perches on my right shoulder—this one's wearing a very stylish navy blue business suit—does she have a blouse on under that jacket?—with a contemporary red briefcase swinging from her hand.

"I hired a local artist to do the mural..." Natalie says.

Furious Flat Julia is off and running... how the hell much did we pay for this? she demands.

"In exchange for classes for her daughter."

Impressed Flat Julia has taken over the lead.

"I'm amazed at what you've done here," I say to Natalie.

A tentative smile reappears. "Really? At first you looked... angry."

"I think I am just a bit in shock," I say. Gone are the folding chairs I had for the waiting parents. Instead, there are a variety of black wooden chairs lined up neatly against the wall, all with the same silver material on the seat pads.

"I had an old dining room set in my garage so I took the chairs and made seat covers. Then I went to a thrift store and got a bunch of different wooden chairs and painted them all black. I bought ten yards of the silver material to make the seat cushions the same, tying the chairs together."

"Very creative."

Furious Flat Julia and Impressed Flat Julia start whining in stereo on my shoulders. "I'm supposed to be the creative one here," they say, suddenly possessive of the toy we had dropped in the sandbox that we were tired of playing with.

"If you're the creative one," I ask Flat Julia, "why didn't you do this?" I am getting really good at carrying on one conversation in my head with Flat Julia, and not losing track of the conversation that is happening in real time.

Before Flat Julia can answer, Natalie says, "This is nothing. Wait until you see the office."

I freeze. My office? Furious Flat Julia is jumping up and down on my shoulder, ready for war.

I walk slowly behind Natalie, peering into the office, and breathe a sigh of relief. Natalie isn't dumb. She left my desk exactly as it was, in exactly the same place. She has added a small desk, smaller than mine I note, on the side wall where the filing cabinets used to be. I don't ask where they are. I don't care. My desk is still in the front of the line.

"All the paper records have been stored in the basement," she says. "It's all on the computer now."

That's when I notice my junk table off to my right, which was normally covered with leftover costumes that I planned to donate to a children's hospital, single ballet shoes that were waiting to be claimed, and class attendance books that needed to be filed. Pretty much a junk table that I tried not to look at.

Now the table is empty except for a computer, complete with a twenty-five inch flat screen monitor.

Impressed Flat Julia takes a swing with her stylish red leather briefcase and beheads Furious Flat Julia.

"Oh... my.... God," I say, wheeling my chair over to the computer and sitting down in front of it. "All my records?"

"All done."

"Every student has her own file?"

"Yes. With all her pertinent information."

"And payments? The payments," I gulp—the ones that are going to take me all summer to record?—"are in here?"

"Yes. Each and every last one of them."

"What about—"

"The outstanding invoices?"

I nod. There has been a time or two when a new season has started in September and I didn't even look back to see if anyone owed payments from last year. I've probably lost millions.

"Invoices have already been sent out." Natalie wheels her chair over to me. "I know the summer isn't very busy for the studio..."

Well, maybe this summer isn't going to be. She has already done more than I ever accomplished in any previous summer.

"I think we could up the enrollment of the summer program..."

I am listening, but really just want to play with the computer. Julia Stone's Dance Academy computer!

"...by having a mini-recital at the fall kick off."

Oh God. Doesn't she know I need a full year to recover from the recital business? That it is blasphemy to even talk about the recital for at least six months?

"Of course it wouldn't be as big as the year-end recital, so we could do it in the studio. It would give the girls a reason to keep taking classes during the summer."

I start breathing again. In the studio might be do-able.

"And," she says, sounding more excited, which almost scares me. I'm pretty sure if I get more excited about something than I am about the computer, I will probably have a heart attack and die.

"I think in the fall we should offer ballroom classes. For the parents. I know all the moms want to do it, so we just need to convince the dads. We've got our very own market right here, in the studio. We can do a mailing. And we could have a ballroom demonstration at the fall kick off."

Add more classes? Add a whole other style of dancing? I take a deep breath. Wait a minute. I'm the dance director. Flat Julia answers for me. "Funny. I was thinking the same thing." I grin. "And maybe Phillip and Dan could dance for us then."

"Julia..." Natalie says, ready with her logical arguments.

"I know."

I have to admit... it's nice having someone else to blame for the tough decisions.

With Madelyn's crazy advice swirling in my head... have an affair with myself...

and visions of my new studio...

and Flat Julia's sudden inspiration—she's taking full credit—of adding ballroom dancing to Julia Stone's Tap Academy...

I feel oddly lost, and inspired, all at the same time. I put the top down on my car and start cruising. I end up at my condo because... well, because I don't know where else to go.

As soon as I walk in the door I feel embraced by this beautiful space.

There's no music. No phone. No television.

No noise. No demands. Nothing needs to be done.

I turn on the tall stained glass lamp that Angela let me "borrow". Dragonflies are captured in gold and brown hues, their iridescent wings, so fragile in life, are strong and bold.

I sit on the big comfy couch that looks and feels like giant marshmallows. If I had a white couch like this at home, I certainly wouldn't let anyone with food or drink anywhere near it. But it's not mine, it's from the rental company. And it's only me, and my little cup of coffee, so I sit. And do nothing.

Breathe.

Sip.

Breathe.

Sip.

The condo feels like a finished *to do* list.

I feel like I've never been here before. Not the condo, of course, but at the end of a *to do* list.

It's finished. Complete.

It's heaven.

I don't know how long I sit here, breathing and sipping. Eventually, I notice my Time-Out doll still leaning in the corner, her head resting on her raised arms. Something isn't quite right. I go over and tilt her head so she is looking over her shoulder into the room, just like Katie used to do. I can almost hear my little Katie asking, "Is my time up? Can I come out and play now?"

That's one big difference between kids and adults. When a child gets punished, they pay their dues, and as soon as it's over, they forget about whatever they've done wrong.

Not like us adults. We keep punishing ourselves over and over, for the same thing. And we never, ever forget the things we've done wrong.

I sit back on my heels. There's still something off with my Katie doll.

Then it hits me. When Katie was little, it never occurred to her that things were supposed to match in color, in texture, or in style. She never confined herself in a box that way.

I can't quite bring myself to take apart my first doll, so I pull the box of doll limbs out of the closet. I dump the whole box out, making piles on the plush carpet. I don't think about it and don't have a plan, but without the pressure of to dos, and shoulds, and need tos, I start.

And before I know it, I have three dolls assembled. "I didn't realize it would be so easy," I mumble softly to myself.

"You just had to find the time," Flat Julia says.

Note to self... no one is allowed into perfect condo without written invitation. Including imaginary friends.

"And space," she says.

Space! I so need space.

"It's like a puzzle," she continues in my head. "In order to get a handle on the whole picture, you need to lay all the pieces out before you start."

She's right. I unpack all of Katie's old clothes and hang them in one closet so I can see them all. I don't want to just pick an outfit and put it on a doll. Anyone can do that. I want to put each doll together with love so they gain a personality.

That's what I remember about Katie. I would buy her a little pink outfit with a matching skirt and top and when she dressed herself, she would never put them together. She would always get something that made me cringe, like a neon orange shirt with polka dots and pair that with the pink skirt. Two items that screamed they didn't belong together.

She would add the black beret hat and her little black cowboy boots she insisted on wearing the whole year she was two. Winter, summer, it didn't matter. She needed her hat and boots. Somehow the black on top and the black on the bottom tied it all together and suddenly orange and pink did match.

I make myself learn from her. I take the matching T-shirt off my Katie doll and hunt through the closet until I find the piece of clothing that would normally be the last thing I would put with the pink skirt, and I make myself put it on her. Of course, being a sentimental mom, I had saved the beret and boots.

Two hours later, I stand up and stretch. In three corners of the living room, I have prototypes of Time-Out Design Dolls.

My cell phone rings and I fish it out of my bra and answer it without thinking. "Hi, Julia. It's Angela. I've got good news."

I put what's left of my coffee in the microwave.

"We've got an offer," she says.

"An offer?" It sounds crazy, but I forgot that she's actually a realtor and not an interior decorator.

"On the condo," she says.

"Of course," I answer. The condo. An offer on the condo. My condo.

"They are offering twenty thousand less than what we asked for."

"Twenty thousand dollars less?" Haven't they seen the condo? They should be offering twenty thousand dollars more.

"Remember, it's a first offer," she says. "We can go back and make a counter offer."

I look around. My haven. My dolls. I feel like I have finally carved out a little space for me in my life. I'm afraid if I sell it, I'll never find it again.

"We could meet them in the middle," Angela says.

"You said with all the staging, we would probably get the asking price."

"What about Time-Out Designs?" Flat Julia asks.

I look at my dolls, the ones that are made and the ones that are waiting to be made. I imagine putting the pieces back in the box.

"If you pack them up, you might as well throw the whole box away."

"Dammit!" I don't know if I'm talking to Flat Julia, or to Angela.

"It's totally up to you," Angela says. "We can play hardball. If they really want it, there's a chance they'll meet it."

"I think we should wait a bit longer and see what happens," I say.

"I'll call their agent and let them know you're firm on the price."

Me? Firm?

"I guess I am," I say to Angela. I smile, feeling like one of my dolls peeking out over her shoulder into the world. *Am I done being punished? Can I come out and play now?*

Chapter Twenty-Two

Michael and I are in bed, having a picnic, otherwise known as a truce or a cease fire on our last conversation. We used to do this every Friday night. We'd get pizza, half pineapple for me, half plain cheese for him, and we'd jump into bed and watch "The Sopranos". Sometimes we even had sex on commercials only. We'd start on every commercial break, and as soon as the show came back on, we had to stop. That was the rule.

Our show got cancelled, and somehow we forgot about commercial sex. "I got an offer on the condo today," I say.

He pushes pause on the remote and leans over and gives me a kiss. "That's great, babe."

"They offered way too little."

"It's just negotiation. You go back with a counter offer, then they make another one. Eventually, you both give a little."

"I don't want to give."

"You've got to give. Everyone has to give a little. You can't get everything you want."

"Why not?"

"Because life is about compromising."

"I don't want to compromise." I take the remote and press play. "And I'm officially starting the doll business."

"The one you and Charlotte have talked about?"

I nod.

He presses pause again. "I didn't know you two were talking again."

170

"We're not." I don't add that I think about calling her every day. That she is like my tree in a forest—if something happens in my life and I don't tell her, did it really happen?

"Don't you think you should wait for her?"

"Wait for her? She moved to North Carolina to be with Ken, remember?"

He just looks at me. Maybe he and Tinkerbell are having an affair. Or at least they're commiserating and sharing strategies.

"Fine. Of course I'd rather do it with her. But if we can't, then I still want to do it."

"You guys will make up."

"How do you know we can get over this?" I press play, mumbling under my breath but loud enough for him to hear. "There are a million things you could do that I wouldn't forgive you for."

He laughs. "Yeah, well, there's nothing you could do."

Now it's my turn to press pause. "You're full of shit! You don't know. What if I became an alcoholic?"

"I'd send you to rehab."

"What if I had an affair?"

"I'd lock you in the house so it couldn't happen again."

I press play. He's got an easy answer to everything. I lie down and pull the blankets up to my shoulders.

"Julia, why do you find it so hard to believe that I love you, no matter what?"

I, who never have the easy answers, say what I know he wants to hear. "I believe you." And I do—I believe he believes it. This is his first serious love relationship and I don't blame him for being naïve. I lace my fingers with his, wishing I could be naïve again.

I lie on my side of our bed, listening to Michael breathe. I don't remember how this became my side of the bed, but it's marked as clearly as I'm labeled an independent on my voting ballot.

How come a conjugal bed gets divided into sides? I wonder. Isn't splitting the bed in two the opposite of what sharing a bed is supposed to be about? Sides, clearly marked, like country lines. Borders. Boundaries.

Michael wiggles up behind me. I feel his erection disrespecting the hedge between my side and his side of the bed. His chest hair tickles my back. He pushes my sweatpants down over my hips.

I try to go with the flow. Try to find the river of acquiescence that has become part of my personality. The problem is the river starts out like a smooth ride in the moment, but I have realized it actually leads to a waterfall that will pitch me over the edge, completely unground me, toss me and turn me until the world doesn't make sense anymore, before I finally crash onto the ground below and get battered and beaten by water the weight of rocks.

I scramble out of his arms. "I can't do this anymore."

Michael sits up, glancing at the door, ready to play hero. He thinks someone is attacking, mistakenly assuming the attack is coming from the outside. "Do what?" he asks, looking confused.

"I can't do this anymore," I repeat, scrambling out of bed, standing on my side of the bed, a yellow satin war zone between us.

"Do what?" Michael asks, getting out of bed on his side.

I parry his question with one of my own. "What are we doing?"

"I thought we were going to have sex. Then maybe watch some television. And fall asleep. Not a big deal." He picks up his pajama pants, clearly frustrated that his well-planned evening has been interrupted, like a favorite television show that gets cut off by the bleep of the cable company... this is a test. This is only a test. If this were a real emergency...

"Not a big deal?" I pull up my sweat pants. "You're right! Us having sex is not a big deal," I say with so much sarcasm I can taste it. My tongue feels like a razor in my mouth, full of cruelty, wanting to hurt someone else instead of me.

"That's not what I meant," he says, resigned because this isn't going to be easy. He couldn't just cross sex off the list of plans and skip to a little television and falling asleep. "Of course it's a big deal."

I watch him scramble in that way that men do when they're clueless... when they have no idea what they've done wrong. When they think it must be that time of the month when an unpredictable beast has replaced their wife. I hate him for scrambling. *Engage the beast!* I want to roar. "I don't even know why we're having sex anymore."

"Because we love each other," he says.

It absolutely amazes me that he believes it's that simple.

Amazes me. And then enrages me. Does he really think a stupid Hallmark card is the answer? I don't want platitudes. I want blood.

"How can you be so stupid?" I stalk to the back of the bed, crossing to his side. I mimic him in a disgusted voice, "Because we love each other." I choke on my own venom. "Do I look like I love you?"

And then I sit on the bed and cry. Hurting him doesn't make me feel any better. My pain is like a boomerang—I shoot anger at him but it only comes back to bite me, peppered with layers of guilt.

"Babe, what is wrong?"

I can smell his desperation as he asks the question, sitting on the corner of the bed, close... but not too close, with the caution of a soldier ordered to cross a field of landmines. A part of me feels for him, but a bigger part of me is jealous. He has the option of disobeying the order, of going AWOL.

For me, there is no escape. I am the landmine. "Are we trying to get pregnant? Have a baby? Or are we just finding that loving feeling? I mean what are we doing?"

"Why can't all that stuff, loving you and having a baby, all be the same thing?"

"Really? That's what you're going with? It's all good?" I cry. "All you have to do is kiss me and I start doing math in my head. Sixteen days since my last period. Since my average cycle is between twenty-four and twenty-seven days, it would be eight to eleven days until my next period. And at noon on day eight, I'd decide I was pregnant. But too soon to test. Day nine I'd be looking at baby clothes. Day ten I'd start to worry about risks to our daughter or son, depending if it was an even or an odd month because we would have a boy if it was an even month and a girl if it was an odd month, and what is August anyway? Even or odd? Even or odd? Suddenly I need to know. And by then, you are done. And I lie there, my legs sticky, wondering how you couldn't know."

"Know that you had faked it?" he asks.

"No." *Are we even speaking the same language?* "How you couldn't know if we were having a boy or a girl." He's looking at me the same way I've looked in the mirror for a long time... like I've completely lost my mind.

He sighs and tries to put his arm around me. "I guess I didn't get how much this stuff was driving you crazy."

He still doesn't. But he is trying. "I need to know what we're doing."

"I thought we agreed to just see what happens."

Just see what happens? My blood pressure skyrockets, a geyser about to blow the roof off our bedroom. "See what happens? See what happens?" I have to get control of myself. I breathe in and hold it, trying to count to ten. Holding it in doesn't seem like a good idea and I blow the air out of my mouth. "See what happens is what you do with gas prices. See what happens is what you do with the stock market. See what happens is not what you do with a baby!"

"I told you I'm fine either way," he says.

"Fine isn't good enough for me. Having a baby should be something you really want... really, really want with all your heart." I breathe out, not even realizing I was holding my breath. "Or not."

"Babe, I'm fine. Not your fine," he says, "but my fine. I want to be with you. You are my family."

I know I am supposed to feel better... he is saying everything any normal woman would want to hear.

"Do you want to have a baby?" he asks softly.

"No." I thought the truth, the beginning of the truth anyway, would shake our house. Would rock our world. But nothing shifts. *Except everything.* "I'm sorry, I don't. I feel like I should. That if I really loved you, I would. But the truth of the matter is I don't want to start all over. I am tired, more tired than I have ever been in my whole life."

"It's okay," he says. He moves over and this time I let him put his arm around me. If only he could hold me like this forever. I feel like someone has reached inside and turned the relief valve on the pressure cooker that is me. But I know it's only temporary. The truth has begun working its way out like a splinter... *Ready or not, here I come.*

Chapter Twenty-Three

You know the story of Sleeping Beauty? The prince comes along, kisses the princess, and she rises willowy as the wind and waltzes off into happily ever after. Well, assuming the fairy tale is a metaphor, then my body is Sleeping Beauty, Marco is the prince, and dancing is my kiss of life.

Instead of rising like the wind, though, my body is more like the zombies in that old Michael Jackson "Thriller" video. You know, where the skeletons are rising from the dead. Creaking. Aching. And missing limbs.

I'm sweating in my ear canals, stretching from my toenails to my eyeballs like I'm on the rack... and I couldn't be happier.

Marco tightens his hand on my back, the man's universal signal that he wants his dance partner to stretch—more. I swear I can't.

But I do.

About an hour ago, my body stopped listening to me. It ignored my cries for relief, poo-poo'ed my whining, and blatantly told my brain to shut up. It could only have one master and, traitor that my body is, it chose to listen to Marco. Instead of me.

Thank God my body is smarter than my brain.

"The tumble turn is challenging," he admits.

He says challenging. I say downright impossible.

"I could choreograph another step here, but this fits the crescendo in the music perfectly," he finishes.

We try again and I can't get past him enough to allow us to spin together.

"You have to go forward," he says for the twelfth time. "Not sideways."

"I know. I tried."

"Then stop trying."

United States champion and that is his best advice? Stop trying?

"You're stuck in thinking mode," he says.

"How can I not be? You told me to go forward. With my toe. On the inside edge of my foot. With a shoulder lead..."

"Clearly, your mind has heard the techniques." He takes a deep breath and puts his hands on my shoulders, my dance Obi-Wan Kenobi. "The mind has an ego of its own, often repeating itself just to hear itself talk. It tends to hang onto control, leaving the body numb... in limbo."

Body... numb...limbo... Yeah, that place sounds familiar. Like the past decade or so. I don't want to be numb anymore.

"Quiet your mind and trust that your body has received the knowledge. Take a deep breath, release it slowly, and when I count us in, we're going to do it. Ready?"

Hell yes, I'm ready. I feel like I can see the finish line of a hellaciously long race. One I thought would never end. I don't answer him with my voice. I don't need to. I answer him with my body. And I can feel him hear me.

"You've got to trust your body," he says softly, "and let go."

I trust you, my body is screaming. *I trust you!* I've never felt so aware, so achingly tensed up, waiting for the right moment, the perfect moment for release. Letting go never sounded so good.

"Five, six, seven, eight.

Our body, the energy between us touching so lightly we could hold a butterfly captive between us without crushing its wings, takes flight and we are no longer bound by the laws of the universe. A portal has opened up and we are dancing on a single strand of magic between heaven and earth.

I feel him anchor my turn and I soar past him, bringing him with me. Rising and falling in sync, two bodies dancing as one.

A seamless, heavenly, perfectly-executed tumble turn.

I drop into Madelyn's chair, making a mental note to call my health insurance company and find out how I get authorization for more than the ten sessions allowed annually. "You want the good news?" I ask. "Or the even better news?" I know I shouldn't care what she thinks of me, but I can't wait to make her proud.

"How about the good news," she says.

"Okay. Dancing with Marco has been amazing. I really do love to dance. And I really am done with the life of a professional dancer. I just don't have it in me anymore, not that I could anyway, at my age."

She smiles. "Because thirty-eight is so old."

It's probably hard for her to understand because she can be a therapist no matter how old she gets. Her chosen profession is probably like wine... you get better as you age. For a dancer, though, thirty-eight is ancient. "I guess I just put it away when I had Katie. And I was happy to do it. But now that Katie is growing up, I am looking back at what I gave up and thinking I still want it." I lean forward. "Dancing with Marco has made me realize I don't want that part of dancing anymore."

She is quiet, waiting to see if I have more to say.

"I thought there was only one way to dance," I say. "Seriously. Or not at all."

"And you've found another reason?"

"Remember when you told me 'if it's good for me, it will be good for everyone around me'?"

She smiles. "I remember you had a lot of trouble saying it."

"I've got a daughter. And a business. But dancing... I can totally see how in this case," emphasizing that I am not in total agreement with her, "in this case, you're right. Dancing is great for me. I even went to a tap class in Boston. Just because I wanted to. And there were all these women, some were older than me and better than me."

"How did it feel?"

"Putting on my tap shoes, just to dance, was wonderful. Not to teach, or to demonstrate, but to learn. And to remember things I had forgotten I have forgotten. It was great."

"Seems like Marco came into your life at exactly the right time," she says.

"You would love him. He says things like, 'I can't feel you'. So I would touch him more, and he would say, 'I still can't feel you'. Because I was trying so hard to make him feel me, I wasn't feeling me. When I actually only thought about myself, about my center, when I ignored him and what I thought he wanted, he would get all excited, and say that's it. That's the connection I want. I want you to bring you to me."

"Maybe I should have an affair with him," Madelyn jokes.

At least I think she's joking... "He's not married," I add.

Madelyn laughs. "I'm just kidding. We're not here to talk about me."

I pause. "You think life sent Marco to remind me I love dancing?"

"Do you?"

"I don't think the fates are making Marco's coaching schedule," I say.

"Call it fate. Call it magic. Whatever you call it, I think life has lessons and knowledge for us all the time. Every minute of every day, potentially, has great insight. Or awareness. I think that's the human challenge. How much can you find?"

"Like an Easter egg hunt?"

"Sure, little eggs of wisdom hiding in the strangest of places. Places you don't automatically think to look," she says. "So what's the other good news?" she asks.

"You're not going to believe it. I can hardly believe it." I take a deep breath, the words still unfamiliar. "I told Michael I don't want to have a baby."

"Really?"

"Yup. The other night. We were in bed, and the next thing I knew, we were fighting. Or arguing, or whatever. And I... I just said it."

"How do you feel about that?" she asks.

"I feel so relieved. As soon as I said it, I mean, I didn't plan to say it. I didn't think about it. It just came out. And it felt so right. It was like I didn't even really know it until I said it out loud. Like how could I have not known?"

"I don't think you wanted to know," she says slowly. "How did Michael react?"

I picked at a thread on my pants. "Kinda like a man in front of a firing squad."

"Julia, is that what you're afraid of? Are you afraid he won't want to marry you if you don't want to have a baby?"

"Maybe. Probably not. I don't know."

"Julia, stop pretending you don't know how you feel."

She sure is a killjoy.

"You say you love him—"

"I do." I'm never telling her my good news ever again.

"Are you sure about that?"

If my insurance company won't cover today's visit, I'm bouncing the check I give her. "Yes, I'm sure."

"When you married your first husband, was it in your vows that he had to be able to get you pregnant?"

I shook my head.

"So you wouldn't have divorced him if you didn't have a baby?"

"We got divorced, remember?"

"Stop playing games. You're like the street corner magician hiding a coin under three nutshells. Don't you realize you're not doing yourself any favors by hiding?"

"I'm figuring things out. Isn't that what therapy is for?" I am going to answer every one of her dumb questions just to prove her wrong.

She smiles at me sadly. "Do you remember when you first came to see me?"

"Yes. When I got the dance floor."

"And remember where you were before that?"

"The chiropractor?"

"Julia," she says, like I'm an errant child. "Before that? How did you start the day that you couldn't stop crying?"

I honestly don't remember. "Before I went to the chiropractor..." Damn, what was I doing before I went to the chiropractor? I was home, I woke up... "I had sex with Michael," I whisper. "Are you saying I was crying because I don't want to have a baby?"

"I don't know," Madelyn asks. "Were you?"

As I drive to the airport, I decide I am going to have to have a talk with Madelyn. If she's got me all figured out, why doesn't she just come out and tell me these things? Five hundred dollars ago, apparently the first time I came in to see her, she could have told me I didn't want to have a baby. I could have thanked her and left. Hell, I would have given her the cash up front and saved the gas money.

Unless it's hindsight. It's easy for her to look back and put two and two together. And she'd probably argue that I needed to figure these things out on my own anyway.

Who cares? I think, changing the radio station, looking for an upbeat song to put me back in my good mood. She is right about one thing. There is magic around every corner and today, my magic is flying into Logan via American Airlines. Katie's coming home and I can't wait to hug her, squeeze her, and touch her sun-warmed skin.

Let's test Madelyn's theory that we could know things if we just stopped ourselves from not knowing. I want to hear Tina Turner sing "You Better Be Good to Me." Since it isn't on any of the radio channels, I flip the switch that turns the power on the five disc CD player in my trunk. One of the CDs I put in the trunk player was Tina Turner's Greatest Hits. Five CDs, with roughly fourteen songs per CD would give me a one in seventy chance of hearing that song. Before I hit play, I pull over into a rest area and take a moment to put the top down, knowing that I want to drive down Route 93 with the wind blowing in my hair singing at the top of my lungs with my girlfriend Tina. I take a deep breath, hit play, and pull back into traffic. I hear the CD player shuffling the CDs.

The drum kicks on and within two beats, Tina is jamming and I am right there with her. "You better be good to me!" I scream into the wind. "That's how it's gotta be!"

It isn't until the song is almost over that I remember I am testing Madelyn's theory of magic. Okay. The second song I want to hear... is...

Bon Jovi... "It's My Life."

Tina finishes, takes an imaginary bow in my head and leaves the building.

And believe it or not, Jon Bon Jovi takes the stage and his voice floats from my car up toward the heavens. "It's my life... It's now or never!"

I never knew "knowing" could be so much fun!

I park at the arrival gate. Since we didn't know which gate Katie would be coming in, we agreed I would wait right here. I tap my fingers on the steering wheel, looking into the crowd, dying to see that blonde ponytail bopping up and down.

I forget all about the test as I scan the crowd. At first, there are only a few stragglers. Then a big crowd comes out and I know her flight landed twenty minutes ago. Just enough time to get their luggage, so she should be coming out any second.

The very second I see Katie, way in the back of the crowd, the third song comes on.

Michael Buble... *Home.*

My DNA pulls me toward her like a magnet and I jump out of my car. I am halfway to her when she sees me and for one second I think I probably should have waited in the car. But my heart flips when I see her drop her bag and run toward me like the final scene in the movie "An Officer and a Gentleman" when Debra Winger and Richard Gere finally realize they are meant to be together forever. I catch Katie in my arms and swing her around like I did when she was little.

"Mom, I missed you!"

Her words are sustenance that will get me through six months of teenage moodiness. "I missed you too, sweetie."

We gather her bags, say good-bye and lots of thank yous to Emily's family, and climb into my car. "So how was Disney?" I ask.

"It was amazing. The rides were awesome. And we went to this really cool water park on the hottest day we were there. And there was one roller coaster Emily and I wanted to go on every day, but the twins didn't like it. And Emily's mom wanted us to stay together as much as we could."

Of course she did. The-family-that-plays-together-stays-together mantra she's always saying.

"But that meant every time we wanted to go on the roller coaster," Katie said, "we had to go on 'It's a Small World' again, 'cause that was the twins' favorite ride."

Is that dissatisfaction with the perfect family I hear? "Didn't you like 'It's a Small World'?"

"I did. The first time. And even the second time. By the third time though, I just wanted to bop all those little characters on the head like whack-a-moles. I know you like Emily's mom and everything," Katie says, "but she's a bit like a cheerleader on speed. She never stops talking, and she would never leave us alone. If you had taken us, I'm sure you would have let us go off on a couple of rides by ourselves."

I nod. No way am I going to talk too much. Not now. Not while I'm in the lead.

"Emily's always saying how lucky I am to be an only child, and I tell her she's lucky to have sisters. But after this trip, Mom..."

I hold my breath.

"I kinda get what she means."

I ask, real casual, "You do?" praying she'll elaborate.

"Just that it's kinda nice to have all your attention. Not always," she says with a grin, "but most of the time."

I control myself. I really do. I want to scream for joy but I know better. I keep both hands on the steering wheel as we drive home, but inside I'm waving them over my head in victory. Katie likes me better than Perfect-Mom-Tina!

Chapter Twenty-Four

The very last thing I do before I go to bed—after I check that the doors are locked, after I brush my teeth and put on my night moisturizer (when I remember and, based on the face I saw in the mirror tonight, I'd better start remembering more often) is check on Katie. I turn on the hall light so it shines softly into her room. Sometimes I watch her for only a few seconds, just long enough to make sure she is breathing. Other nights I stay a bit longer, always grateful that God or Goddess gave me this child. I figure I've had just over five thousand nights of this ritual. Five thousand sounds like a lot. Five thousands dollars is a lot of money. Five thousand pairs of shoes is heaven. Five thousand moments of knowing with absolute certainty that your baby is okay is...

...*not enough*.

Sometimes I take her picture, wishing I could stockpile this feeling. This moment at the end of the day when she is tucked in safely and all is right in my world.

If I could capture the feeling, I'd find one of those tiny bottle necklaces, the ones from the olden days when women would wear smelling salts around their neck, and I'd wear it, my personal feel-good balm.

I sigh, almost wishing she would wake up from a bad dream and insist I lie down with her. She'd only been gone a week and that's been long enough to throw my compass off. How am I going to handle college?

My cell phone vibrates for two seconds, indicating I have a text message. Since Michael and Katie are the only ones who text me, I know it has to be from him. I look at the screen. "Come Away With Me."

As I walk downstairs, I hear Nora Jones' sultry voice singing ... "Come Away With Me."

Our song. The first song we danced to.

Little did I know how symbolic that song would be for our relationship. Here was this very attractive, younger man, interested in me... and it felt so good. He still had that oh-so-seductive faith that life will be an adventure. Our first dance was full of promise and he unwittingly pulled me back over to the dark side... back to when I believed in things like "love will conquer all" and "life is fair."

Back to before I knew life was never that simple. Love can't conquer all. Bad things do happen to good people. But it is so tempting because I like believing those things.

And it seemed so safe. Because he was younger, my mind said there was absolutely no way this could go anywhere. So my brain took a break... and my heart took over. But my heart had no safeguards, no check points. Given free rein, I fell in love with him.

By the time my head came back on duty, it was too late.

I was head-over-heels in love with a man my brain didn't approve of.

I am so caught up in the memory that when I get downstairs, it takes me a minute to notice what is different. The plastic that has been up covering the door to the den ever since I had sent the contractor away was ripped off. Light flickers through the doorway making shadows dance on the floor.

Michael is standing in the den. On the finished wood floor. Candles are everywhere. On the windowsills. On the shelves. He even has a polished brass candelabra standing in the corner with two big pillar candles.

Nora keeps on singing. "Come away with me, in the night."

"Can I have this dance?" he asks, reaching for my hand.

I don't know where to look. At the floor. At the amazing job he has done secretly finishing the room... or at him.

So I start crying.

This room seems to have that effect on me.

And Michael lets me. He comes over to me and takes my hand, bringing me further into the room. He gently folds me in his arms and does the one and only step I taught him so long ago... a basic foxtrot step that he does to whatever song was playing. It doesn't matter that this song is a waltz, Michael does the only step he knows. The one I taught him five years ago when an old friend had asked me to teach her bridal party to dance at her reception dinner. Michael was one of the ushers, the only single man in the wedding party, and we paired up for the class.

"You like the floor?" he whispers in my ear.

I can't remember what I had decided about the floor—did I want it or not?—but who cares? I have the floor because I have Michael. Michael... who lets me cry and doesn't always need to know why. Michael... who finished the floor that I had wanted all my life. Michael... who remembered the first song we ever danced to.

Michael, who I had told I didn't want to have a baby, is still here. "I love it," I say softly. "And I really love you."

"You know what I think?" he asks.

"What?" I ask, lost in Michael's arms, hoping I'll never need to be found.

"I think," he continues, "we've talked about getting married a bunch of times. I think you should have a ring." He pulls a velvet jeweler's box out of his pocket.

I hold his hand between mine. "Michael, this is too much. The floor, the ring. It's too much."

"There's never too much of a good thing," he says.

There it is. The difference between us. He really believes there couldn't be too much of a good thing. I, on the other hand, know there can.

He stands up, taking me in his arms again, and I am grateful for the contact. Moving with him, I am tempted to drift off on the current of us ... dance with him, agree with him.

"Julia, do you want to marry me?" he asks, hypnotic, to the beat of the music.

I step out of his arms. This is how I get in trouble; taking the easy way. "It's not about what we want..."

"I'm okay with whatever happens. You are the beginning of my family. And you... are... enough," he says. "We've got everything tied together, like a big old house of cards. Are we going to have a baby? Can we have a baby? Because of our age..."

"My age," I correct.

"Our age, together, we'd better hurry up. Hurry up and know everything. I don't need to know everything right now. You told me you don't want to have a baby. And I'm okay with that."

"You might get it now, while you're twenty-nine. Most of your friends haven't even thought about having a baby yet. But they will. And then what? When it's too late. When you're married to a woman who, by then, couldn't even if she wanted it. Then what, Michael? Then you leave me? Or worse, you stay. You stay and resent me. And you'll resent that I have Katie. So then while I still love you, you'll slowly start to hate me."

"Julia, I get it. We've decided we aren't going to have kids. We said we could think about adopting, or fostering, if we both want to, in a couple of years. When both of our businesses are a bit more settled. The timing is perfect for both of us."

I want to believe him. I want to believe he can be so sure. "What if you change your mind?" I ask.

"I'm not going to."

I feel like he is so determined to get me to say yes that he isn't recognizing the choice he's making. I feel words sticking in my throat, a tug of war between what I should say—and what I don't want to say. *If you marry me, you'll never have kids of your own.* It's one thing to say it in my head, and God knows I'm doing the best I can to run away from the truth inside myself, but once it's out there...

We'll have to deal with it. And dealing with it means he'll have to leave me. And I don't want him to leave me. Half of me wants him to understand that he is choosing me over his future children. The other half of me is screaming to ignore the elephant in the room.

I move back into his arms. "It's so not fair," I say softly. I can take care of him and have a baby. Or take care of myself and not have a baby. Love shouldn't put your needs in contradiction to the needs of the people you love.

I can't look at his face as I whisper, "If you marry me, you'll never have kids of your own."

There. I've said it.

He holds me away from him, forcing me to look at him. "Julia, when you said you'd marry me when you got pregnant, I started trying so hard because, well, because it was fun, but underneath it, I think I was afraid you wanted my baby more than you wanted me."

I blink. How could he have thought that? Apparently, there's more than one elephant in the room.

"So when you said you didn't want to have a baby, in one way, I was relieved. Now I'd know you're marrying me because you want to."

"You know I want to be with you," I say. "We don't need to be married. What does a piece of paper prove?"

"It proves that I'm enough for you."

Him? Enough for me? Not only is my elephant in the room, apparently there's a whole herd.

"It's one thing if your girlfriend doesn't want to have a baby," I say. "It's a temporary condition. At your age, it could be years before you decide you want them. Years that we can be together.

But if your wife doesn't want to have a baby, it's a life sentence."

He looks at me like one of the elephants is about to sit on me. "How can you think marrying you is a life sentence?"

"Because it is," I insist. "You're making a life choice by marrying me. A choice to never have children."

And just then, my bra starts ringing.

Chapter Twenty-Five

"**A**re you going to answer that?" Michael asks, staring at my shirt.

"Of course not," I say, fishing for the phone in my bra. It feels like a timer going off... like the phone is one of those sticks in the turkey that pops up to tell you when it's cooked. A timer beeping out a warning... my eggs are cooked, my heart is old. Even my bra is tired of multitasking.

"Your boobs are calling," he says with a smile.

I try to smile back as I play hide and seek with the phone but my fingernail scratches my nipple and I curse. Unhooking my bra and catching the liberated phone all at once, I swear I will burn this bra and any other in my drawer that's over ten years old.

I hand him the phone and gesture for him to put it on the shelf behind him. "Can you shut it off for me?" I ask.

"It's kinda late for someone to be calling," he says. "Don't you want to know who's calling?"

"Katie's tucked in, you're right here, no one else matters."

He starts to press the button on the side, then stops. "I think you might want to get this," he says, passing the phone back to me.

"Why?"

"It's Charlotte."

I take the phone and stare at the caller ID. Her name and her cell phone number are on the display. Did the palpitations of my heart send her a text message telling her I am sorry from the bottom of my soul?

"Julia," Michael says, "answer the phone."

My fingers are shaking as I open the phone. "Hello?" I say with a question, afraid she isn't really on the line.

"Julia...?"

My heart cracks at the sound of her voice.

"My mother's had a heart attack."

"Oh my God."

"The doctor said it was mild. I just landed at Logan airport and I'm on my way over to the hospital. I know you're probably still mad at me—"

Mad at her? "What can I do?"

Charlotte starts crying, her breath ragged. "Will you meet me at Boston Hospital?"

"I'll leave right now."

Charlotte sighs. "Julia, I'm so sorry."

My nose starts running and I pick up my discarded bra and use it as a tissue. "I am too, Charlotte. I'm sorry for everything."

By the time I hang up, Michael has my purse and coat ready. He hands me his car keys. "Take my car. It will be warmer than your convertible."

"Katie—" I start to say.

"I'll take care of everything."

"I'm supposed to give her a ride—"

"Then I'll give her a ride." He helps me on with my coat. "You just go."

"Michael, I'm sorry. We were in the middle of talking—"

"Go find Charlotte. I'll be here when you get back."

There's something about meeting someone at the hospital in the middle of the night that puts everything in perspective.

I walk down the stark hallway. Why are hospital corridors always painted white? There is probably a color at the paint store called Hospital Corridor White—one that makes your heart race and your stomach drop. One that makes you remember that your world can change in an instant. That the little things really don't matter.

Another thing to add to my list of things-I'll-never-get-to... petition Benjamin Moore to come up with a new color for hospital walls.

Because hospitals aren't just a bad place. People come here to give birth. To get healed.

And to make up.

Charlotte calls me in the car on my way here: her mother is alert and talking and the doctor says she is going to be fine.

She says I don't need to come.

I tell her I'm coming anyway.

She tells me not to rush.

I do.

She tells me she doesn't need anything.

I'm bringing her a coffee—extra cream and sugar—just the way she likes it.

I see her in the waiting room, and she looks up as I come down the hall. We walk into a hug like we've never been apart. I feel like I am on one of those waterslides, with tunnels that twist and turn and you can't see anything until finally, at the bottom, you drop into the pool and remember that you can touch the bottom.

"My mother's going to be fine," she says. "My father's in with her, getting her moved to a private room. They want to keep her for one night, just for observation."

"She's lucky she has both of you," I say as we sit down, and I hand her coffee as I have a million times before.

I don't know what to say, don't know what she needs, so I reach over and take her hand in mine.

"Ken's not here," she says.

I try to read her, but she's blank. She doesn't say anything else. Probably doesn't trust me not to judge. Based on my past behavior, I don't blame her. "I'm sure he has a good reason," I say.

"Yes. I told him not to come."

I smile. "That's a good reason."

She looks at me. "But I don't want to go through this alone."

"And you don't have to."

"Aren't you going to say he should be here?"

"Not if you told him you don't want him to be."

"Don't you think if he really loved me he would ignore me and come with me anyway?" She looks at me. "I told you not to come, once I knew Mom is going to be okay, but you came anyway."

I'm not sure what to say. Do we expect the people we love to do what we want, know what we want, even if we never tell them?

"Don't you think if I really love him," Charlotte insists, "I would want him here? I wanted you here."

I smile. "That's different."

"Why?"

"Why?" I repeat, stalling. "Because..."

"Wanna hear something funny?" She takes a sip of her coffee.

"Sure," I say.

"She looks like me."

"Who?"

"Ken's wife. Well, his exwife."

"Apparently he likes the gorgeous type."

"No. I'm serious. She looks like me... ten years ago."

"Huh?"

"She came first though, so maybe I look like her," she says, leaning her head back against the wall. "What I'm trying to say is she's younger than me."

"I thought you were the younger, hotter woman?"

"Well, you're partially right. I'm definitely younger and hotter than him. But she's younger and hotter than me."

I sit there for a minute. "Since he's older than you, maybe he realized she's too young for him."

"Are you sticking up for him?"

"No. I'm sticking up for you. As I should have done all along. I always wanted what would make you happy, but I thought I knew what that was better than you did."

"And you don't think that anymore?"

"I wasn't right, Charlotte. You went for it, you tried, you had the guts to go to the table and take a taste." I sigh. "I just stare at the buffet like a picky kid, saying I don't like this and I don't like that. Until there's nothing left except the tablecloth. Then I martyr myself, eat it, and pretend to be surprised when I get a tummy ache."

"Yeah, well, guess what? You were right."

I lean forward, still holding her hand tight in mine. "What do you mean?"

"As soon as I got there, I knew I didn't want to be with him. I don't want to be his new, well his old, wife."

"What did you do?"

"I got in the U-Haul and drove to Myrtle Beach."

"You've been at the beach for the last few weeks?"

"I couldn't stay there. And I didn't want to come home and admit what an idiot I am."

I squeeze her hand. "The most important thing is you tried. You gave it a chance. If you've decided it's not the right thing for you—"

"But that's the whole point, Julia. I didn't try."

"Of course you did. You rented your apartment, got a manager for your business, and moved down there."

"It looks like I tried. On the outside. All that drama, and the flair of it... packing up my life to go be with the love of my life."

"Exactly."

"On the outside it's all romance and irresistible love."

"What was it on the inside?"

"On the inside, I only wanted him if I couldn't have him." She starts laughing. Deep, soul-wrenching laughter that can only lead to tears. "And the reason I am this way is lying in that bed in there." Her laughing and crying were doing their dance of grief, circling each other, trying to decide which emotional reaction would win. "I spent my life trying not to be my mother."

And the tears won. "When I was thirteen, I made a promise to myself," Charlotte says, holding her hand out for a tissue.

I hand her one from the box on the table beside me. It's practically empty—what kind of hospital buys small boxes?—and I have a feeling we are going to need more.

"I swore I was never going to be like my mother." She takes a deep breath. "My father has a mistress."

I don't know what I expected, but that certainly isn't it. We are sitting in the hall right outside her mother's room. "Maybe we should move down to the waiting room."

"She knows."

"Who? Your mother?"

"Yes. She knows. She's known longer than I have. And I've known for over twenty years. I was thirteen when I saw him with her. I spent a month, going back and forth. Should I tell my mother? Should I not tell her? And then one night at dinner, he said he was going on a business trip and it just came out. I called him a liar."

"Charlotte, I'm so sorry." I can tell—in her mind she is back at that table. "What happened?" I ask.

"My mother slapped me. Right across the face. It was the only time either of my parents ever hit me. She told me not to talk about him like that."

"But what did she say about the other woman?"

"She wouldn't let me tell her. Said she knew all she needed to know." Charlotte shakes herself. "When I went down to North

Carolina and looked at Ken, I realized it was the safeness of him being married that allowed me to immerse myself in the idea of loving him. I've been living my life, my whole life, trying not to be my mother."

"Charlotte, I'm so sorry."

"I thought if I wasn't the wife, if I was the other woman, I'd have everything I wanted." She sighs. "But I can never find what I want, as long as I'm basing everything on not being something else."

She looks over at me. "We're opposite sides of the same coin."

"What do you mean?"

"You're living the shoulds. And I'm living the should nots."

She's right. How the hell did we, two intelligent women, end up living our lives based on what we were taught we *should be*, directly or indirectly? Just as important as the message of what we should be... are the messages of what we shouldn't be.

No wonder it feels impossible to be authentic. Should and should not. Do and do not. Internal and external voices. And the external voice backs up its advice with threats... if you do this, then that will happen. And everyone knows you've got to avoid "that" at all cost.

"Let's make a deal," she says. "I promise to listen to you every time you see me about to do something I should not. And I'll promise to tell you when I think you're doing something that you think you should."

I reach out my hand to shake. "But what about when I'm going to do something I shouldn't?"

She takes my hand in hers. "I promise to cheer you on all the way!"

She's as incorrigible as ever. "What are you going to do now?"

"I'll make sure Mom is settled and then give Dad a ride home. Then I'll go back to my condo."

"I thought you rented it?"

"That was the plan. Lucky for me, it hasn't happened yet."

"Charlotte, you're here in the hospital with your mom, you have more issues with your parents than I even realized, and you've just uprooted your life for the second time in a month. I love that you can say you're feeling lucky."

"You know all it will take to be a trifecta?" she asks, a serious look on her face.

"What?"

"Tell me you'll meet me for coffee Monday morning, as usual."

Thank God hearts can heal. Her mom is going to be fine. Our friendship is going to be fine. And I've got a coffee date for Monday with my best friend in the whole world. "I'm driving back from New York Sunday night. I'll be there!"

Chapter Twenty-Six

I zip up my small suitcase and look at my watch. Ten minutes until Eva picks me up.

"I wish I could come to New York," Michael says, leaning against the door in our too purple bedroom.

"I do, too," I say softly, walking into his arms.

"I feel like I'm picking Katie over you."

"Welcome to parenthood. Believe me, I hate missing her softball banquet."

I can feel him grinning in my hair. "Yeah, sure you do. You've been to one of these every year for the past five years."

"Yes. But this year her coach is particularly hot."

"If I wasn't the coach, and this wasn't Katie's last year..."

"Just so you know," I say, "she says that every year."

"Whatever. I'd much rather come to New York with you."

I hug him tight. "I wish you could come, too, but I'm glad you're going to be with Katie. I feel guilty enough not being there myself."

"We'll be fine," he says. "I'll video the banquet, and you video the show, and we'll have a family movie night when you get back." He looks at my suitcase. "That's a pretty small bag. Do you have got a costume in there?" Michael asks.

"Phillip swears the dress his partner had made for this number will fit me."

"Well, knowing Eva, she'll have three backups, just to be safe."

"I'm counting on it."

"Babe, I thought a lot about what you said the other night," Michael says.

"About?"

"About how you don't want to have a baby. How you think you're too old to be pregnant."

My man... the slow cooker. Just when I think he isn't listening to me, or that he hasn't heard a single word I've said, he'll come back to the discussion table.

"And you also seem to be afraid that someday I'll be sorry. That I'll look back and blame you."

Wow. He really *was* listening.

"I've come up with the perfect answer."

I didn't really know there was an answer...

"Adoption."

I think my slow cooker has blown its cover clear off.

"I called my friend who adopted and got the name of his attorney."

I drop onto the bed and try to catch my breath. Baby steps. One thing at a time. Isn't that what Madelyn is teaching me to do? "Michael, I only just realized I don't want to have a baby. I want to live with this for a bit before we go start making the next decision. I feel like you're pushing me."

Hell, he isn't pushing me. He's already started taking steps without me. He's way ahead of me and he's trying to drag me along with him.

"I'm not saying we do it tomorrow. I'm not even saying we need to adopt. I want to take away your worries. And I want to marry you. Julia, you're an amazing woman and I feel lucky to be with you. But truth be told, I also feel like it's the kind of luck that has an expiration date. I'm sick of waiting for my time to run out."

Eva honks and it's time to go.

What are the chances two men in my life will lose it on the same day?

Apparently, very good.

The final rehearsal for the show is going fine. Phillip and Dan are dancing their tango, and it's even more amazing seeing it the second time. It is our turn to dance next and Marco walks over to the DJ to give him our music. While he's gone, I peek at myself in the mirror again. Male dancers, even if they aren't gay, certainly have an eye for clothes. He promised that his partner's dress would fit me, and it did. Like a glove. Soft chiffon, in a million of shades of blue, cascades down my body.

That's when I hear the DJ say to Marco, "I'm sorry, sir. I don't have a cassette player."

That's when Marco loses it. It's like he walked slowly down the pier, took off his designer clothes, folded them neatly, then jumped straight off the crazy dock.

"What do you mean?" he yells. "When I hired your company, I very specifically said I would need a cassette player for the show."

"I'm sorry. My boss never told me. I have one at home—"

"What good is that going to do?" Marco yells back. "This is our song. It's the only copy I have. We have to dance to this song!"

I walk over to Marco and touch his arm. "It's okay, Marco. We've got plenty of time to run out and buy a CD before the show."

"What about rehearsal?" he asks.

"I can sing," I try to joke.

Eva, who has been watching from the back of the hall, comes forward. "I've got it on my iPod," she says, pulling it out of her purse.

"Why do you have a copy of the song?" Marco asks, amazed.

"Because..." she says. "I just do."

The DJ takes the iPod and connects it to his console.

"Leave it to Eva to save the day," I say as we take our place behind the curtain off-stage, waiting for our turn.

"She certainly saved my ass," Marco says quietly behind me.

"Marco, why this song?"

"It was my wife's favorite song. She used to ask me all the time, would I still love her tomorrow?" The first few notes of the song fill the room. "And I always said yes."

"Marco, that's beautiful, and sad, at the same time."

"I know. Who could love me when I'm still in love with a ghost?"

I look out at Eva and suddenly it makes sense. Why didn't he ask Eva to dance with him? Why did she always seem busy when he was around. "Maybe someone with her own ghost," I say softly. I look at the poster on the side of the stage that has a picture of his wife. I know she wouldn't have wanted Marco to give up on love. "What if I told you I think your wife broke your partner's ankle on purpose?"

"What?"

"You said she tripped on one of the signs for this event. That it was a fluke accident. What if it wasn't an accident?"

"My wife does not go around hurting people."

"Maybe her ghost does. Only for good. So that you would come to Eva's studio. She was trying to get you together. And you picked me instead. I think she's pissed. I'm not dancing until you agree to give Eva a ride home."

It is almost time to go on. "Fine. I'll drive her back to the hotel after the show."

"Oh, no. I mean home. I'm not driving home with her. Not with your wife pissed at me."

"She's not pissed at you."

"Okay. She's pissed at you. She wants you to love again. And I think she's picked Eva for you." And I happen to agree they make the perfect pair. I can't believe I didn't think of it earlier.

"Fine. I'll drive her home."

"On your motorcycle. I happen to know she loves motorcycles."

"You want me to drive her from New York to Boston on a motorcycle?"

I've done my part. If his wife's ghost knows what's good, she'll whip up a thunderstorm that will force them off the road. Into a hotel. With only one room left. "That's exactly what I want."

It's one thing to think about visiting the past.

It's a whole different thing to take a step back into your own history as a dancer, with hundreds of people watching.

I peek out into the ballroom. The elegant theme of the evening is evident in the white tablecloths and the black napkins folded like flowers at each setting. Black and white balloons decorate every corner of the room. Most of the men are dressed in tuxes and the women in sophisticated evening gowns.

Eva and Marco are the only ones dancing on the small floor in the center of the room. She is glowing in a cream-colored gown. Pearls hang in strands across her back, barely holding the dress in place. In his dark tuxedo, he is her shadow as they sway to the dinner music.

It's moments like this that I believe in serendipity.

That feeling is almost enough to calm the butterflies that have come to live and breed in my stomach.

Phillip rushes over. "I need help with my tie," he says in a panic.

Seems someone else has butterflies, too. "Where's Dan?"

"He's doing this meditation thing he does. I had to get out of the room. The chanting music was driving me crazy."

I fix his tie the best I can and he rushes to the back where a large ornate mirror leans against the wall. He undoes his tie.

"I'm not a five-year-old who needs his dirty sneakers tied," he grumbles. "I need a professional. Where's Eva?"

"Eva is busy," I say. "You leave her alone."

"Why? Where is she?"

He follows my eyes and sees Eva dancing with Marco. "Well, I'll be damned," he says with a soft whistle. "Now," he spins me around to face him, "fix my tie."

I try, but I don't know what I'm doing. "You're bouncing too much," I say in my defense as he walks off in a huff, mumbling under his breath that women really aren't good for much. In this case, I happen to agree.

I stand still amongst the commotion of backstage. There's a vibrating energy, a blend of nerves and excitement, as dancers stretch and stage hands get various props ready. I use a wire brush on the suede bottom of my satin dance shoes to give me a little extra traction.

I don't remember being this nervous for a show. Not since my very first tap solo. Eva had come backstage to wish me luck, a huge bouquet of pink roses in her arms. When she saw how nervous I was, she dropped down on her knees in front of me. "What's the worst that can happen?" she asks.

"I'll forget all my steps," I whisper, afraid just saying the words would make it more likely to happen.

"Do you really think it's the steps that are important?"

Of course it was the steps. I spent almost a year learning my solo routine.

She rubs her hands up and down my arms. "I'll let you in on a little secret," she whispered. "Dance isn't about the steps."

"It isn't?" I ask. It was like she was confessing the secret of Santa Claus—not that he was real—and not that he wasn't. That truly, as we all know somewhere deep inside, the truth lies somewhere in the middle. "Then what is dancing about?" I whispered.

"A true dancer has the dance inside of her, like a little secret. And her job on stage is to let the beauty of that dance shine through," she said.

"I thought I'm supposed to do my dance just the way I learned it," I said.

"Most of the time. But sometimes a dancer has to dance what's in her heart right at that moment. And every once in a while, her heart tells her she has to change the steps. That for her to truly dance the song in her heart, she has to dance something else."

"You're saying I can do whatever I want on stage?"

Eva smiled. "I'm saying that you have to trust yourself. Your teacher has taught you everything you need to know. And the rest is up to you. It's your body and your dance. Are you brave enough to share your dance with us?"

"So it's okay if I mess up? If I forget?" Even at six, it was hard to let go of the idea that there was only one right way to do something.

"That's the point, Julia. It isn't forgetting. It isn't messing up. If you end up doing something a little different than you've done before, just make sure you do it with all of your heart."

Too bad I hadn't learned that lesson in life, too. Eva is right. In dance—and in life—going through the motions just isn't enough.

I walk over to the big mirror. Marco's partner's dress fits like a glove. I run my hands over the soft material of the blue dress. My body looks like it's crying as shades of blue cascade down my body in material soft as air. The light reflects off the dark blue rhinestones that glide like rivers of tears down the bodice and scatter sparkles of light all over my skirt.

When did life become about getting everything right? When did I stop believing that trying your best is enough? When did I start judging myself against a perfect ruler, always coming up short?

Now I'm terrified I'm going to do it all wrong. I won't know what beat to start on... I'll forget to stretch my ribs... I don't remember how to share my joy.

What am I thinking? I can't go out there and dance—

"Babe."

Michael?

I see him in the mirror, standing close behind me. I turn and throw my arms around him. The butterflies in my stomach welcome him, as if sharing has set them free.

I didn't even know I was missing him, but now that he's here, filling one of the holes in my heart, I realize I've been missing him for a long time.

"I can't believe you're here," I say, muffled in his shoulder. My dress envelops him.

"I couldn't miss this chance to see you dance," he says, holding me tight.

I pull back a fraction. "What about Katie and the banquet?"

"Katie's staying with Emily. I did the coach's speech before dinner, then drove like hell to get here." Michael squeezes me. "I'll be right in the front row," he says.

"I think those seats are all taken," I say, not wanting to let him go.

"Eva said she'd save me a seat." We peak out from behind the curtain and sure enough, there she is in the front row, with an empty seat beside her. Her question echoes across time. *Am I brave enough to share my dance?*

Michael kisses me, careful not to mess up my lipstick. "For luck," he whispers. "Not that you need it," he says over his shoulder as he walks down the side steps.

I take a deep breath. At the end of the night, I may be sharing the dance with Marco, and sharing my heart with Michael, but I can only share what I have.

First, I have to find my body. I line my body blocks up as Marco taught me... slightly roll my hips under so they are a solid foundation to support the rest of my body. Then the ribs. The glorious ribs. Was it only a few weeks ago that my ribs felt stuck and rigid, a stifling cage around my heart? Tonight I can feel the subtle shift and sway that I've been practicing and the protective shell around my heart loosens.

I focus on my breath, appreciating the air that fills my lungs and relishing the relief of letting go. I am grateful to the tips of my toes that I have been able to resuscitate my love for dance. Just when I had come the most undone, the most unraveled in life, I found the dropped thread of dance. By weaving its passion back into my heart, a quivering pulse of desire to be whole again has filled my soul.

Marco appears at my side. "We're next," he says. "You ready?"

No! Yes!

He takes me into dance position and we shift slowly from foot to foot. As we move together, slowly, as we breathe together, I know I won't be out there alone. He'll be with me... literally, every step of the way.

Trust.

This is what it means to dance with someone. This is what it means to love someone.

Trusting they will be with you for the perfectly executed steps... and the stumbles.

I trust Marco to dance.

And Michael...

Roberta Flack's voice whispers out of the speakers and we float to the center of the stage. *Tonight, you're mine. Completely.*

The spotlight warms me. Music comes up through the floor as if a twenty piece orchestra is playing beneath me and a serpent-like power spirals up through my body. At last I have found my hibernating joy and believe, once again, that I have something worth sharing.

Adrenaline, butterflies and emotions course through my body.

You give your love. So sweetly.

I remember why I fell in love with dancing in the first place. Dance welcomes passion; my joy... and my pain. It shoves aside "nice" and "pretty" feelings and demands honesty. Only raw emotion will make the dance come alive.

Tonight, the light of love is in your eyes.

A fountain simmers in my core, deep inside where my spirit rests. As the music builds, the fountain grows higher, spraying gold dust inside my body like bright stars in a dark universe.

For the final dip, I lift my ribcage as Marco lowers my body. Stretching up as I go down. Breaking me open.

The song fades and the audience comes to their feet clapping for us. Looking out, I have eyes only for Michael. He deserves honesty.

Something I've been afraid to give him.

Roberta Flack sings the last haunting refrain...

But will you still love me... tomorrow?

Chapter Twenty-Seven

Back in my hotel room with Michael, still in my dress of tears, I take Michael's ring out of my suitcase. Half of me wants to throw it out the window, fling myself into his arms and refuse to ever leave this room, even knowing that by denying the past, I extinguish the possibility of a future.

I can't even think about marrying him until he knows everything. And once he knows everything, there's a very good chance he won't want to marry me. But if he's willing to make the choice never to have kids to be with me, then he deserves the truth.

Five years ago, I faced two choices. Swallow the poison and hope I would survive. I pushed it into the darkest corners of my heart where I never looked at it, pretended it didn't exist, hoping I could go on as if it never happened.

But I've learned the hard way that the secrets in your heart leak out into your blood, your body, your soul. Secrets contaminate everything.

The second choice was honesty. The unadulterated fear of honesty is that it will have exactly the same effect, that it will cost me everything. My secret has already ruined the past and stained the present. I am terrified it's going to cost me the only thing I have left... the future.

"Julia—" He steps towards me, his arms ready to enfold me.

My stomach is swollen, infected with my own secret, and I taste bile. It is killing me to hurt him. There is no easy way to say this, no words that can soften the blow. "I had an abortion."

"What?" He stops several feet from me. His face is blank, like he can't process the words I just said.

"Two months into our relationship—"

His jaw drops open and his eyes widen as comprehension bleeds his face white. "With me?"

Would it be easier if I were confessing to a transgression in college? A mistake from so long ago that he could believe it wouldn't touch us? Whether it would be easier or not, it's not the truth. I close my eyes and nod.

"The night the condom slipped off?" he whispers in shock.

My heart stops on a contraction. He remembers. I always wondered if he even remembered that night. "I got pregnant," I say, the words tearing open the scars in my heart. "And I had an abortion."

He is frozen in place, staring at me. But his eyes—his beautiful blue eyes—are drowning... he is crying.

"Two months into our relationship, I didn't know we would keep seeing each other," I say, trying to defend the indefensible. "I had the abortion because I loved Katie and was afraid I didn't have enough in me to be a mom again by myself. And I didn't want to trap you. But then we started getting more serious. And then we talked about having a baby. And when we tried, we couldn't have one."

He sits down and rubs his eyes. "That's why you did it..." He is looking around on the floor as if he can find enmeshed in the carpet some semblance of the world as he understands it. "But why didn't you tell me?"

"I didn't know what to do."

"But you did know what to do." His hands are shaking, pain and anger simmering in his body. "You decided this without me. You went and..." He looks up at me suddenly. "Did someone go with you?"

"Charlotte."

"You told Charlotte?" His anger boils over. "It was just me you didn't want to tell. Me... the only person who had a right to know." He's straddling a frantic seesaw of hurt and anger. "You and Charlotte decided, when it should have been you and me." His feelings flood the room and I try to squeeze myself into a corner.

"I needed a ride home," I say, knowing every word I say is inadequate.

"You wouldn't even ask me for a ride home?" His shoulders droop as if the weight of my betrayal is too much for him. He looks like a different man. Older. Sadder.

"How could I ask you for a ride when I couldn't tell you what was happening?" I move to sit beside him.

He jumps up, a volcano of anger erupting. "Don't you dare say you couldn't! Don't you dare put this on me! You could have told me. You should have told me!" His face is flushed as his heart floods his body with rage. "I meant nothing to you. Our baby meant nothing to you."

My heart is breaking inside my body and stabbing me with its sharp edges. "Oh God, that's not true!"

"It is true."

"It was early. I got it done as soon as I could."

He looks at me as if I am stranger. "What does that mean? That it doesn't count?" He stands up, stiff, as if I've broken something inside of him that can never be fixed.

"Of course it counts. It's been with me every single day."

I can tell he is desperately trying to reconcile who he thought I was five minutes ago with who he thinks I am now, juggling balls of fire he doesn't want to catch. "Do you need me to forgive you?" he asks.

"I... I don't know. It was an accident!"

"Getting pregnant was an accident. Having an abortion... that wasn't an accident. That was a choice. And not telling me? That wasn't an accident either. You chose not to tell me."

"I tried to do what was right for everyone at the time."

"No. You did what was right for you!"

"I'm sorry. I am so sorry."

He stares at me. "What are you sorry for?"

"I'm sorry for not telling you."

"Are you sorry you had the abortion?"

"I am sorry, but..."

"If you had to go back, would you do it again?"

"Yes, but—"

He slams his fist onto the dresser dismissing the rest of my words. I don't even know if they matter anymore. "But I should have told you." I have done it. Finally taught him one of the terrible lessons of life... that it really is the people we love who can hurt us the most.

"Why are you telling me now? Why now?"

I am silent. I know he thinks it means I don't care. But what else is there to say?

"Julia, goddammit! Answer me! I deserve an explanation. Why are you telling me now?"

"Because you should have a chance to walk away," I whisper the words.

"I'm not the one looking for a reason to walk away."

"No. Not until now."

He stares at me. "You won't even try to stop me?"

I shake my head slowly. "No. Now you get to decide. I've been dealing with it for the past five years."

"No, you haven't! You haven't dealt with it. You've hoarded it, like a secret. You've saved it and now you're using it against me. "Why?"

"I told you..."

He cuts me off. "You want me to leave. Is this my punishment for the condom slipping off? For not knowing I got you pregnant?"

He doesn't need to be punished...

"That's what you want. I can't believe it." He picks up his jacket.

"Don't go."

"It's what you want, remember?" He opens the door. "All this time I've been asking you what you want. I should have been asking you what you don't want, because you've been screaming that answer for a long time, and I just didn't want to hear it."

I have no right to ask for anything but I beg anyway. "Please don't go."

"You've been telling me what you don't want," he says, walking toward the door. Tears stream down his face as he whispers the final note in a sad song. "Me."

Chapter Twenty-Eight

I collapse into Madelyn's chair and hand her the letter Michael left for me on the kitchen table when I got back from New York.

Julia,

I took your key to the condo and I'm moving there for the next couple of months. I'll still pay my share of the mortgage on the house.

Michael

Madelyn hands the note back to me and I fold it carefully before putting it back in my purse, right beside the velvet box with his ring.

"What happened?" she wants to know.

I swallow. Saying it out loud isn't getting easier. I can't look at Madelyn so I stare at the painting on the wall of a little girl blowing a dandelion, her wishes scattered on the wind. "I had an abortion five years ago. I didn't tell Michael then, but I had to tell him before I could marry him. So I did. And he left."

I peek through my eyelashes. Madelyn hasn't moved. "That must have been quite a shock for him," she says.

I feel a spark of anger in my belly, but it is quickly extinguished by gallons of acid guilt.

"And quite a burden for you," she says gently.

"I don't have that burden now. And I don't have Michael." I sigh. "Telling him was absolutely terrible. It's like I have this grotesque sore inside my heart, festering, that I never wanted anyone to see. Telling him was like giving him a magnifying glass to see my ugliness." I can still see the sterile room. The stark white walls and the blank white face of the doctor. My decision left me without the right to see color. I want to cry, but poison has hardened my well of tears. "It didn't hurt as much as I thought it should."

"You wanted it to hurt?" Madelyn asks.

"I deserved for it to hurt." Toxin is boiling inside my well, hiss and steam from my soul. "I wanted it to hurt more than birth. I wanted my blood splattered all over the walls."

"That obviously didn't happen," she says softly.

"No. I had some cramps. And that was it." I sigh, the weight of the world on my heart. "I was sure everyone would know because I felt branded. How could Michael not know? It was written all over me." I finally look at her. "And when he didn't know, I figured out why."

"Why couldn't he see it?"

Inside, I am numb. "Because a part of me disappeared that day right along with what could have been."

Madelyn leans forward. "Julia, I would say it hurt you."

"It didn't hurt enough," I say softly.

"There's a difference between physical pain and emotional pain. Don't you think the pain your soul has endured is enough to make up for the physical pain you didn't feel at the time?"

"To be honest, I don't feel anything right now."

"I don't believe you," Madelyn says. "You lost a piece of your soul." She leans forward some more. "That's not quite right. I think as self-punishment, that piece of your soul turned and has been tormenting you for five years. And you want me to believe you don't feel anything?"

I stare at her, wondering if she's gone mad. "I thought therapy was supposed to make me feel less pain?"

"Feeling nothing isn't the goal, Julia. I'll support you in growing and learning and understanding yourself. But I won't support you in pretending everything is fine."

I jump up. "I've done everything I can. I told Michael! What the hell do you want from me?"

"I want you to feel," she says.

I stand behind my chair, aware the purple velour is an inadequate defense from Madelyn's probing. "You won't be happy until I fall apart."

"I don't want you to fall apart. But Julia, you've seen how not dealing with this has been hurting you and your relationships. Don't just go halfway. Go deep inside. To every part of your being. Are you ready to deal with it there?"

I pace around my chair. "Okay, fine." Pacing around the chair is making me dizzy and I start walking bigger circles around the couch. "Abortion is legal. It's done in a regular doctor's office. It's a simple procedure. It's a right women have fought hard for. A right I do believe in." As I say this, it rings vaguely familiar. Apparently, this is a subconscious litany I've been telling myself for five years.

"Everything you are saying is completely true," Madelyn says, "but I think it's only your head talking. How does your heart feel?"

I stop in my tracks. There's nowhere left to run. "That day I betrayed myself," I say, dropping onto the couch. "Even though, if I had to go back, I'd probably do it again. But that day changed me." I take a ragged breath. "What I did goes against everything I believe about myself. Although I do believe abortion should be legal, it was never supposed to be an option for me. Never, ever something I would do." I feel blackness penetrate my body like an ink stain. "And I did." I wrap my arms around myself, shaking in my own embrace.

"Julia, your heart isn't about right and wrong, Pro-Choice or not. Your heart only knows what it feels."

I grab my neck like a person choking. "My throat hurts," I whisper.

"It's okay," she says calmly, moving over to the couch to sit next to me. "The neck is the bridge between the mind and the body. There's a lot of trauma there." She wraps her arms around my body and I cling to her. I am afraid I am going to disappear.

"Julia, your body embodies the soul. Your soul is talking to you. You just need to have the guts to listen."

"I'm scared."

"What are you afraid of?"

"I'm afraid if I take down the stone wall that's in my heart, I won't be able to stand."

"You built that at the time to protect yourself. But it's time to take it down. It's also imprisoning you."

"It hurts. It hurts so much," I cry.

"I know," she murmurs softly, close to my ear. I pretend I am her voice... that I am listening to my body.

For a moment, time stops as I finally bear witness to my pain.

"And Julia..."

Uh-oh.

"You know telling Michael is only part of it."

I know I should run. Leave. And never come back.

"You thought you had to be punished. Do you think the abortion is why you couldn't have a baby?" she asks.

Her question pierces my heart through the one tiny opening in my wall. Stones crash down from my heart into my stomach, slippery with anguish, avalanching me with grief. Pain explodes in my body and, for the first time in five years, I know why I am crying.

Words tumble out of me. "One time I said no to a pregnancy. And then when I said yes, life said no."

Madelyn holds me. "Maybe you could have carried the guilt of the abortion around with you for the rest of your life. But once you added the grief of the miscarriage, I think it was more than your soul could bear."

Tears wash down my face, onto my blouse and hers, and I don't even try to hold on anymore. It's too late. I am on this emotional landslide and there's nothing I can do.

"Julia, you need to feel the grief. And stop feeling the guilt."

I look at her. "How do I do that?"

She smiles sadly and shrugs. For once, I believe she wishes she did have the answer for me.

Chapter Twenty-Nine

I am nervous about telling Katie that Michael has moved out. I have no idea what her reaction will be. I worry about how the instability of my relationship will affect her... now and later.

I rush around the kitchen, trying to create a casual environment. When she was little, sometimes after school I would buy lots of fruit and we would cut it up together. Her little fingers would pick the seeds out of the watermelon. And we would have fruit and warm croissants for dinner. So this morning after therapy I went to the grocery store and bought lots of fruit. Our hands will be busy and we'll be able to talk. Mostly, I'm hoping she will feel stuck in the kitchen. Otherwise, I'm afraid she will listen to me tell her he's moved out, then go to her room and I'll never know what kind of emotional damage I've caused.

The croissants are in the oven, the fruit is on the counter, and I'm sweating.

When I hear her coming up the stairs from the garage, I grab the grapes and turn the faucet on full blast.

"Oh, brother," Katie says, dropping her bag on the floor just inside the door. "What is it now?"

"What do you mean?" I ask, wishing I had changed into a loose T-shirt.

"Last time I came home and you had fruit, you wanted to talk about birth control."

"Can't a mother have a nice snack for her daughter without having an ulterior motive?" Damn. I do have an ulterior motive and she just gave me an opening. Which I missed. I wish I could forget this whole conversation, give her money to order a pizza, and go to bed.

She picks up a knife and starts carving the pineapple. "So... there's nothing you want to talk about?"

"Well, there is something."

"Mom, I told you I'm going to get my math grade up next year."

If only it were that simple. "I know, Sweetie. This is about Michael."

She stops cutting and looks directly at me.

Michael's going to be staying at the condo for a while? We're taking some time to figure things out? "You know, no matter what, I love you. And he loves you..."

"We're moving out?"

"No, sweetie. We're just going to take some time..."

She studies me for a second then picks up her knife again, cutting the pineapple into perfect squares.

"So why did you kick him out?" she asks.

Who said I kicked him out? "Michael and I have some things to figure out—"

She cuts too hard and one of her squares is mashed. "Mom, I know it wasn't his idea to leave."

Actually, it was. But not really. "Why are you so sure it was my idea?"

She continues cutting, not looking at me. Not giving anything away. "Sometimes I think I like him more than you do."

Thank God I'm not holding a knife or surely I'd be missing a few fingers right now. "How can you say that? Half the time you act like you can't stand him. Like his very being annoys you."

"It does. Half the time he does annoy me. Other times, though, like Florida, he helps me out. But I'm honest. When I like him, I like him. And when he's annoying me, he knows he's annoying me."

She finishes the pineapple and moves onto the cantaloupe, scooping the middle out like a surgeon. "But you try to act as if you always like him. Just like you do with me."

I pluck grapes off the vine. "But I do always like you."

"No, you don't. You love me all the time but sometimes you don't like me. Just like I don't like you all the time. But it doesn't matter 'cause we're stuck together. Whether you like me or not, you're my mom." She starts hacking off the tops of the strawberries. "But you're not stuck with him. And since you're so busy pretending everything is perfect all the time..." She cuts the strawberries in half and adds them to the bowl. "You live with him so you must like him more than half of the time, right? But you won't marry him, so maybe you don't."

That's my fourteen-year-old's take on romance? Like your partner more often than you don't?

"I'm not surprised," she says. She takes her fruit bowl and the whipped topping into the living room and turns on the television. I stand at the sink, holding the dripping grapes. Her words are honest.

Her indifference terrifies me.

I am afraid she learned it from me.

Chapter Thirty

I stand outside the door to my own condo, a peace offering pizza balanced on my arm. Do I knock? Ring the bell? Use my key and just go inside?

Michael answers the dilemma for me by opening the door. He's wearing jeans and a linen shirt that's unbuttoned; his feet are bare. He stands in the doorway, not moving aside to invite me in.

I should tell him that I'm sorry and I never meant to hurt him. I should tell him I never wanted him to move out. Instead, I say, "Thank you for taking your shoes off on the new carpet."

Thank you for taking off your shoes? Am I an idiot?

"Julia, what do you want?"

I lift the pizza box, as if he can't see the big cardboard square between us. "I brought pizza. I thought maybe we could talk."

He doesn't budge. "About what?"

"About... everything."

He moves aside. "You? Want to talk? That's a first."

Can you blame me for not wanting to talk? I can't trust what I'm going to say. The man I love has moved out and the first thing I say to him is a polite comment about protecting the new carpet.

I go in and put the pizza on the kitchen counter. I realize I don't have any plates or even paper towels. Then an awful thought occurs to me. What if he's already gone out and bought plates? Somehow that would make it official and I know I can't eat. "I didn't tell you about what happened because I wanted you to break up with me," I say. Not the greatest way to start, but better than shoe talk.

"Why did you tell me? Why now?"

"Madelyn thinks I was punishing myself. That I felt guilty. And although at the time, I thought I was doing the right thing for everybody, looking back, I guess I did feel like a martyr. And then the miscarriage compounded my guilt. And the fact that I hadn't told you made it worse."

He folds his arms across his chest, still standing near the door, ready to open it and kick me out at a moment's notice. "Is that Madelyn talking, or you?"

"She's helped me."

"I am glad you have Madelyn to talk to," he says. I hear the rest of his sentence, the part he didn't say. *But why can't you talk to me?*

His arms fling out and he quickly pushes his hands into his front pockets. "I've been trying to wrap my head around it. Trying to imagine what you felt then. But all I can think about is how I feel right now."

I step toward him. "Tell me."

He starts pacing in the living room. "Tell you? Tell you? Why would I tell you anything? You haven't trusted me in five years."

I try following him. "And we're both saying maybe that was wrong."

He turns so fast I almost crash into him. "Maybe?" His face is turning red. "You're still at maybe? Maybe you should have told me you were pregnant? Maybe you should have told me you were getting rid of our only baby?" His face is such a deep red it's almost purple. "You should be begging my forgiveness for not telling me."

I step back. "You can sit here now and act noble." I feel the question burning my gut and I try to swallow it... the question I know I should never ask...

Words come out of my mouth, against my will. "What would you have done?" I whisper. "If I had told you, what would you have done?"

There it is. The question I don't want to know the answer to.

But maybe I need to know. Would things have been different?

Now I am trembling in the small living room. "Back when you were still calling before coming over, even though I told you that it was okay to just drop in—but you always called anyway," I say. "Back when you were still eating pineapple on your pizza because that's the way I like it."

Michael leans against the wall, his arms hanging at his sides. Like he can't stand being with me in this room anymore. "Julia, why are you here? What do you want?"

"I had to come. We can't just..." I don't know how to finish the sentence. I won't finish the sentence.

"You think now that your conscience is clear, we can just live happily ever after?"

Kinda, yeah. I lift my shoulders and reach toward him. "That's what I'm hoping." I pull his ring out of my purse, the black velvet box burning my palm.

He stares at it like I've pulled a poisonous spider out of my purse. "What the hell are you doing with that?"

"I don't know. I thought maybe..."

"So if I ask you to marry me now... your answer is yes?"

Oh, God. I can't even think about marriage, but if that's what it takes to get him back...

He moves toward me like a hunter closing in. "Everything has been on your terms. And for the most part, that's been okay. But I'm not going to be easy on this one. I want to know I'm the best thing that ever happened to you... well, almost a tie with Katie."

He is standing over me and I am trapped against the wall. "I love you," I say. Even as I say it, I know it's not enough.

"That's not enough. How do I know it's even true? I want more than you love me. I want 'I love you, can't live without you, you're the best thing that ever happened to me' love you." He leans over me. "Can you say, besides Katie, that I'm the best thing that's ever happened to you?"

I'm frozen in place.

"Or are you saying yes out of relief that you've now told me your terrible secret?"

"Michael, please—"

"Are you here because you really want to marry me? Or is this just damage control?"

I honestly don't know.

He grabs my face in his hands and kisses me, hard, possessive, and somehow dismissive all at once. He takes the ring box off the counter and shoves it in my purse. "I don't want it back," he growls. "But I don't want you wearing it, either."

Chapter Thirty-One

Apparently, Madelyn has decided the time has come to take her kid gloves off.

"What does Flat Julia think of the abortion?"

"And a fine howdy-doo to you, too," I say. Damn this woman. Once, just once, why can't she say what I want to hear, and not what she thinks I need to hear?

"Julia, if you want me to coddle you, just say the word."

I half-smile. "Word."

She takes a deep breath and lets it out slowly. "Seriously, what does she think?"

"I haven't talked about it with her," I say sarcastically, adding, "You do know she's not real, right?"

"I know she's not real, sitting here as a third party. But I do believe she's a part of you."

"Great. Well, she's a part that really doesn't need to know about this."

"Can you even say her name and abortion in the same sentence?"

"Who cares?"

"I think you should. And I think she does."

"Talking to my inner imaginary child about this would be the same as telling Katie."

"No, it wouldn't be. Katie hasn't grown up. Flat Julia has."

I sit there, still.

"You felt like you had to tell Michael."

"He had a right to know."

"Why? Five years ago when it happened, you didn't feel like he had a right. What changed?"

"We fell in love. Love changes everything."

"Is that why you didn't tell him in the beginning? Because you didn't love him, or trust him enough?"

"I've thought a lot about this. I think the reason I didn't tell him is because I didn't trust myself."

Madelyn repeats what I said as a question. "You didn't trust yourself?"

"I was afraid he might say he wanted it. One nod from him, this man I barely knew, and I was ready to put my life on the line. Katie's life on the line. He could walk away, change his mind, but I couldn't. Katie couldn't. So I didn't tell him."

These confessions tear my soul out. I feel like my skin is sunburned and the chair is slowly peeling it off. "Then we fell in love, and moved in together, and started trying," I say. "Trying to do exactly what I wanted. Exactly what I had taken away from us. When I miscarried, I was sure God was punishing me."

"How long are you going to beat yourself up for this?" Madelyn asks.

"It was a mistake. Not because we were careless. Not because we were irresponsible. The condom slipped off. That's the one part that still makes me so mad. We were careful. We were responsible. It wasn't supposed to happen."

"That's one of those lessons you don't like. Bad things do happen to good people."

I stand up. "I hate that. You can do everything right, take all the precautions, follow all the rules, and still get hurt." I lean against the wall. "This could happen to Katie," I cry. "This did happen to Michael." I fall back into my chair, pulling a pillow onto my lap and holding it tight. "And I can't protect them," I whisper, my heart breaking again.

Madelyn leans forward. "And Julia. This happened to you, too."

"If only I had known we were going to fall in love, I never, ever would have done it. If it wasn't for me, we could have the life we both really wanted."

"You don't know the other life would have been better. You're trying to take the best of this life, and combine it with the best parts of another life. You don't get to do that." She stops talking until I look at her. When she's sure she has my attention, she continues. "You could have miscarried. You could have had a sick child. You could have had a perfect child. The only thing you do know, for certain, is that you wouldn't be on this particular road."

I sigh, tasting regret.

"Julia, you and Michael fell in love on this path. You have no way of knowing if you had had the baby that you still would have fallen in love. You would have been parents together, and that's a completely different path. You may not have fallen in love. You'd have a child, but you definitely wouldn't have Michael the way you have had him. You would be different. He would be different."

I feel my spine straighten just a bit, leaning toward her. I feel light, as if she is possibly turning a dimmer switch on in my body. Just a hint of light. "I was thinking we would be exactly as we are, but with our baby."

"I can promise you one thing... you and Michael wouldn't be the same."

Except for this one terrible secret, my relationship with Michael has been really, really good. We could have been amazing. Except for this one secret.

Air is filling my hunched body as awareness slowly fills my soul. "It isn't the perfect life I denied us," I say in awe. "It's being present in the life we've had that I've sacrificed."

Madelyn is nodding up and down. "Exactly." She takes a long breath in and lets it out. "You need to accept the decision and forgive yourself," Madelyn says.

If only... "How?"

"I think talking to Flat Julia is one part. I think she has as much right to know as Michael. Maybe more." Madelyn leans forward. "We've talked before about how depression is the splitting of self. And it seems like we have even found the time in your life when this split happened. There are always different parts of self—the child, the adult, the ego, the mother—and that's good. That's what a well balanced person is, a committee of themselves. But when we split, when we think some parts aren't as important as others, or worse, we think they're enemies, that's when we don't trust ourselves."

I feel light, and heavy, at the same time.

"You've started doing this, integrating all your parts. You did it at the studio and that's why you feel so good about your decision. All parts had their say and you came up with what's best for you."

I sit still and listen.

"All parts of you need to deal with the abortion. And then, all parts of you need to decide what you really want with Michael."

"I'm afraid," I say softly.

"Julia, its okay to be scared." She leans forward. "What did you tell Katie when she was little and she was afraid?"

I remember Katie on the slide at the park, her chubby little hands holding onto the sides. "Don't worry. I'll catch you at the bottom."

"That's all you need. Trust yourself to be there for you. If you really trusted yourself to be there at the bottom to catch you, what would you do?"

"I'd let go."

Chapter Thirty-Two

Faced with the seemingly insurmountable task of forgiving myself, I put the top down and drive to the ocean. The sea has always been the closest thing I have to a church and I am going to stay here until I can go home with something... different.

I stand alone at the edge of the shore. The beach is littered with debris from yesterday's storm. Strands of seaweed dance along the shoreline, stabbed by shards of broken seashells. The line on the horizon between the sea and the sky is an abstract battle of shades of grey.

The wind whips around me like sharp claws ripping at feelings that tear into my heart.

Guilt. Shame. Betrayal.

Bone-deep spiritual weariness.

Fear.

Madelyn is right. In my mind, I dealt with what I did. Logically, I can even explain why I did it.

But my heart has been buried alive in denial.

I need to acknowledge my choice. I need to own it.

Words that have both haunted me and changed me. "I had an abortion," I whisper to the sea. I say them so softly that even I can't hear them.

I wait for one big giant wave to come and crush me.

Nothing.

"I had an abortion," I repeat somewhat louder.

The waves continue their gentle rhythm, in and out, kissing my toes, then retreating. Kiss, retreat.

It's not what I want. Not what I deserve. I walk into the water and kick at the waves. "I had an abortion," I say even louder.

"I had an abortion!" I scream to the vast sea.

I wait for the earth to open up and swallow me.

Again, nothing.

In a whisper, barely audible above the wind, Flat Julia says, "I'm sorry."

Flat Julia, the little girl inside of me, is sorry? She doesn't hate me?

Thunder vibrates in my chest as she says it again. "I'm sorry," she says, begging me to listen.

And I do.

"I had an abortion," I say again, this time adding Flat Julia's words, "and I'm sorry."

Tears stream down my face, tiny drops falling into the ocean.

Flat Julia still believes in forgiveness. She believes when you do something wrong, the best thing to do is admit your mistake and say you're sorry.

"I'm sorry... I'm sorry." I fall to my knees, drenched to my waist. "I'm so, so sorry!"

Suddenly, I hear a voice that's outside of me and inside of me all at the same time, a voice that is me and isn't, say, "I forgive you."

I forgive you?

I feel the two sides of my jagged heart brush one another, touching for the first time in five years. The wound in my heart glows with the beginning of healing. I feel Flat Julia stitching the two pieces back together.

"I love you, Flat Julia," I whisper.

"I know you do," she says with a flourish, closing the seam of my heart like the final curtain at a dance show. "I love you, too."

I have a feeling I won't be hearing her voice anymore, at least not in my head. She is finally where she belongs... in my heart

I crawl to the shoreline, cold water pulling at the sand under my fingertips. I have crossed my own barren desert, descended into my ocean of loneliness, and stumbled up my mountain of honesty. Most of the time, I didn't even know what I was looking for.

The last five years of my life, which in many ways have been wonderful—Katie has become a beautiful young lady and I've fallen in love with Michael—have also been some of the loneliest years of my life. Not because I didn't have people who love me, but because I didn't love myself. When I made that choice, I took a part of myself, my grief, and I put it in a tiny box and shoved it deep in my own attic. And then I tried to move on in my life with a man who was part of that. Essentially, I castrated myself with unresolved grief.

Every decision has a price. A consequence. Trying to ignore my grief split me... like parts of me were scattered on different deserted islands, miles apart, with no way of communicating.

Instead of grieving, instead of catching Flat Julia when she fell off the pedestal I put her on, I abandoned her.

Instead of accepting the pain of a bad decision made for good reasons, I sacrificed faith in myself. I second guessed every decision I made after that. Never trusting myself. Always punishing.

The price has been paid.

What's done is done. I am done. I finally made it to the other side of myself.

I will now honor myself, knowing that my decision five years ago does not diminish me as Katie's mother. Just the opposite. I have given my heart and soul to Katie from the minute she was conceived. My choice will no longer separate me from Katie. It will not dilute my joy in being her mother. Being a mom, being a woman, sometimes calls for tough choices.

And tomorrow morning, I will have coffee with Charlotte. I will tell her about my meeting with Natalie and taking her on as a partner. I will tell her about the Time-Out Dolls I made. And I will tell her how much I appreciate that she loves me no matter what. I will thank her from the bottom of my heart for accepting me, wholly, long before I could.

I remember a few months ago thinking... *This can't be my life.*

And honestly, it wasn't. I was missing from my own life. The last few months have been hard. Opening the door to my inner attic, rummaging around until I found the tiny little box buried in the back, the one I tried so hard not to look at, has been extremely painful.

I thought I was supposed to be strong enough to handle anything. I've learned that sometimes the hardest thing to do is to break down the walls that are holding us up. Inside, I found the fragile part of myself that deserves my love. Inside my heart, my soul has finally come home. I am whole again.

But I can't be whole alone. I need Katie. Charlotte. Eva. And Michael.

I turn around and look down the beach, sensing him before I see him.

Michael!

His dark hair is tangled in the wind and he stops a few feet away from me. "I got your message," he says. "You said you wanted to talk."

"Yes. I have a lot I want to share." I smile, a bit scared. My new self feels wobbly and my hand reaches for his like gravity.

I know deep inside, with gratitude, with wholeness, with acceptance and love... *This is my life!*

About the Author

I started out wanting to be a writer, but took a detour of passion as a professional ballroom dancer. Even when I danced, I couldn't stop my pen from dancing across the page. The first line of my attempted romance novel, "Widowhood is so much more respectable," Destinee thought as she loaded the gun," should have given me a hint that romance really wasn't my niche. Now that I'm in my forties, I am much more comfortable writing women's fiction. I aspire to write my novels like Melissa Etheridge sings... not always pretty, but raw and from the gut.

13872375R00150

Made in the USA
Lexington, KY
24 February 2012